PRAISE FOR ANDREAS MAIER

"An exceptionally gifted talent."

—Katrin Grossmann, *Sächsische Zeitung*

"What should we believe? What can we know? These are the significant theoretical questions that Maier's books raise with great humor, sarcasm, as well as skepticism. . . . A magnificently constructed book."

—Hubert Spiegel, *Frankfurter Allgemeine Zeitung*

"After one's first success it is certainly difficult to write a second book, and more than a few have failed miserably. Andreas Maier has overcome this hurdle with verve and skill."

—Ulrich Greiner, *Die Zeit*

ANDREAS MAIER

U S E N

TRANSLATED FROM THE GERMAN
BY KENNETH J. NORTHCOTT

A NOVEL

OPEN LETTER
LITERARY TRANSLATIONS FROM THE UNIVERSITY OF ROCHESTER

Translator's Acknowledgement:
I would like to acknowledge the help of my friend and colleague Dr. Hildegund Ratcliffe, and, vicariously, of her brother, Hofrat Dr. Kurt Weide of Innsbruck, for help on a number of points of local South Tyrolean topography and life.

The translation of this work was supported by a grant from the Goethe-Institut which is funded by the German Ministry of Foreign Affairs.

Library of Congress Cataloging-in-Publication Data:

Maier, Andreas, 1967-
  [Klausen. English]
  Klausen / Andreas Maier ; translated from the German by Kenneth J. Northcott. — 1st ed.
      p. cm.
  ISBN-13: 978-1-934824-16-0 (pbk. : alk. paper)
  ISBN-10: 1-934824-16-X (pbk. : alk. paper)
  1. City and town life—Germany—Fiction. 2. Criminal investigation—Fiction. I. Northcott, Kenneth J. II. Title.
  PT2673.A375K6313 2010
  833'.92—dc22
                              2010012089

Printed on acid-free paper in the United States of America.

Text set in Fournier, a typeface designed by Pierre Simon Fournier (1712–1768), a French punch-cutter, typefounder, and typographic theoretician.

Design by N. J. Furl

Open Letter is the University of Rochester's nonprofit, literary translation press:
Lattimore Hall 411, Box 270082, Rochester, NY 14627

www.openletterbooks.org

KLAUSEN

The landlord in Feldthurns was later unable to tell anyone with complete certainty whether the guest in question was Josef Gasser or not. He said that the young man had ordered a pickled calf's head and a glass of rosé; he, the landlord of the inn in the lower part of the village, had noticed this because the young man had drunk only a single glass of wine, but had not touched the calf's head, merely peered at it in a very ostentatious and peculiar manner so that he, the landlord, had asked him whether there was something wrong with the calf's head. However, the young man had not paid the slightest heed to his questions but had ordered a schnapps and had, on his part, begun asking questions about all sorts of different things. According to the landlord he gave the impression, as he did this, of being on the one hand quite cheerful and on the other strangely interested. The landlord said that he was a member of the Feldthurns Cultural Society, that he was president of it, that Castle

Feldhurns was a unique place of interest and that, in addition to this, Feldthurns also possessed a swimming pool, and that he was only telling him all this because the guest was growing more and more excited as he listened to him. The guest also asked him once, again without any apparent reason, whether the landlord was Catholic. The landlord said that of course he was Catholic, that all the people in the area were Catholic and that he, the guest, was presumably also Catholic, since he was evidently also from the Eisack valley, and on hearing this the young man's mood became downright enthusiastic. He even clapped his hands. Things went on like this for a while, and then two tourists came in, a German married couple. The guest's face darkened. The tourists ordered bacon and wine, talked about the route they were taking for their vacation, praised the province of South Tyrol, and put a guidebook on the table. They immediately started up a conversation with the landlord, the sole purpose of which was to demonstrate their intimate knowledge of the country. Above all, they had some very detailed things to say about Venosta. The landlord, however, did not know Venosta at all. *You don't know Venosta?* asked the two German tourists in astonishment. The landlord said that he came from the Eisack valley, not from Venosta. Whereupon the two tourists began to lecture the landlord about Venosta and the collective beauties of South Tyrol. The aforementioned guest said nothing for a while, and sat staring at the table-top with a more and more sullen expression. But then he suddenly started talking himself, but of quite unrelated matters. As he talked he once more waxed strangely enthusiastic . . . He said that, in his view, the country had a healthy mentality, especially as far as *development was concerned*, that it was not ruined by the government and by environmental

protection measures to the same extent as, for instance, Germany and
Austria were; at least you were able to build in South Tyrol, for that
was the way things were. The world was there for people, after all,
and that was how it had to be developed. He was an engineer. He
worked at the Cross of Latzfons. Oh! at the Cross of Latzfons, said
the tourist with a knowing look, although he plainly had no knowledge whatsoever of the Cross of Latzfons. The landlord looked at the
guest in amazement. Because, naturally, nothing was being built up
at the Cross of Latzfons; all that was up there were meadows with a
cross placed at the summit . . . The tourist said that in his opinion the
beauty of South Tyrol was also its capital asset and this capital should
not be destroyed; they came down from Münster by car twice a year
and every time they were here they breathed more easily: South
Tyrol was like a second home to them. The countryside had to be
protected: develop but protect, interjected the tourist's wife. Exactly
said her husband. There must be a happy medium. The countryside
must be developed but it must also be protected. If there were too
much industrial construction the tourists would cease coming. So
what was being built up there at the cross? The young guest: A power
station was being built. He himself was the engineer of the Latzfons
Cross power station. (The landlord told a journalist from the *Eisacktaler Tagblatt*, three weeks later, that the strange guest had said this in
the following words, "Engineer of the power station at the Cross of
Latzfons.") Of course we cannot do without electricity said the tourist. The wife: What would the world be without electricity? Unimaginable, Klaus, if we had no electricity. The conversation went back
and forth like this for a while, and it became clear to the landlord that
the alleged engineer was only saying such absurd things in order to

inveigle the tourists into making the most embarrassing statements and self-revelations possible. Everything finished up with the alleged engineer's almost forcing both of the tourists to eat the calf's head. He praised the calf's head as the particular specialty of the house, saying that everyone here ate the calf's head, that you couldn't have been in the landlord's in Feldthurns without having eaten the calf's head, *et cetera*. At the same time, the young man himself had up till then never been seen in the landlord's, or even in Feldthurns at all, and could not, therefore, possibly know the calf's head from the land-lord's kitchen. The couple did in fact order two portions of pickled calf's head to go with their bacon. The landlord had nothing to say about all this. While the supposed Gasser was still sitting in front of his plate without touching it, the Germans ate up the calf's head, an embarrassing situation. Then, according to the landlord, the young man from the Eisack valley left . . . The landlord's mother later insisted that the guest in question was certainly Josef Gasser; she had recognized him immediately, three weeks later, among the pictures in the *Eisacktaler Tagblatt* and on the news, and even then as soon as he came into the landlord's she had had a funny feeling. There was something not quite right about him from the beginning. True, she didn't tell the public all this until after the events had already taken place, and when she was asked why, if she knew everything so precisely, she had not said something about it before, she simply replied that she had, from the very beginning, said *everything*, but no one had listened to her. She had been summoned two or thee times to the police in Bolzano in order to put her statement in writing. A number of people from Feldthurns gathered round her for a while, in order to find out this or that about Gasser (or the person concerned); she even said that shortly after the scene with the landlord she had attached a petition to the altar of Our Lady of Perpetual Help, in the church of St. Laurence, with the aim of averting the fate that awaited them. Others, on the other hand, said that that this petition had actually only been there for a few days before the landlord's mother had started talking about it, that is, not until after the whole affair had taken place, and a false, and backdated, date had been put on it by her, and that all it contained was information that she had subsequently taken from the newspaper. Later on, the landlord's mother kept on telling stories about Gasser, about his origins, his family, his character, and his history, even though she had never seen Gasser before in her life. Everything simply came out of the newspaper and from the television. In the same way, her account of Gasser's alleged entrance into the landlord's differed completely from her son's. According to her, Gasser had talked to her son in an *underhanded* way, had tried to win him over for his *undertakings* (this was what she called them), in that he had first tried to find out about his position and then to form an overall picture of him. Furthermore he had asked him detailed questions about conditions in the locality and, as a way of disguising himself, had said that he was an engineer. Meanwhile, having a big appetite, he had eaten a large portion of calf's head. Then, fortunately, two other guests had appeared, a married couple from Münster, and they had protected her son from even worse, for Gasser had immediately stopped talking about his undertakings and had left . . . The landlord's daughter, Julia, said, on her part, that the guest was certainly not Josef Gasser; he did not even resemble him or, as the case may be, the photographs of him that had been published. Whether the strange and suspicious guest had eaten his calf's head himself or not was soon something that no one could any longer say, and this question—so long discussed and treated at length in the local pages of the *Eisacktaler Tagblatt*—was, for some reason or other, found to be of great importance, and it was later even transformed into a political question. These happenings were, in retrospect, later represented in Klausen as a sort of prologue to the main drama or, at least, played up as such. Possibly, some said, Gasser had been walking up on the mountain, had entered the aforementioned inn, and had become outraged at the tourists, but perhaps, others said, everything had simply been fabricated by the landlord to make himself look important . . . Some could not imagine that what people were saying in a lot of places, namely that Auer had been up in Feldthurns, was right, for Auer only seldom left Klausen until the day of his sudden death, and after he have given up consorting with the people at Ploder castle, he never once left Klausen again. True, it was generally known that on one occasion, in an inn in Klausen, Auer and Gasser had actually said, in fact in the presence of a group of German senior citizens—to whom they spent hours telling a whole string of lies—that they were *engineers at the Cross of Latzfons*, but as that had all been in the newspaper, it was supposed, on all sides, that the landlord had mixed up what he had experienced and what he had read, or, like everyone else, had mixed up what came before and what came afterwards and mangled it all into an inextricable tangle. Finally, a few people even thought that the prologue in Feldthurns was nothing but an invention, a mere combination of the motifs that were hovering in space. At the time, opinions about Gasser and his origins were very divergent. A lot was said about him and a lot more was said later on, and, in the process, people's views about him and his family were radicalized. Gasser was the son of a Klausen shoemaker who, for almost two decades, had no longer practiced his craft, but had just sold shoes. All he had left was a little workbench tucked away in a small back corner where, from time to time, he would glue on soles or insert rubber discs into leather heels. Gasser's father was a quiet man, with a marked squint, who, day in day out, sat around in his one-room shop—which he shut at noon—rode his bicycle the nine hundred meters to his home, ate, lay down on the couch, rode back to his shop around three, locked his bicycle up, opened up his business again, and then sat around until six or half-past, a fate the he shared with all the hairdressers and tobacconists and other independent shopkeepers in Klausen, who all sat around in their shops in the same way. When he was at home in the parlor with his family, old Gasser said almost nothing; he usually reduced every impulse to conversation to nothing, by making sounds like *ach* or *oi*, because everything else was too exhausting for him, it overtaxed him. But when he was sitting in his shoe shop, his greatest pleasure was when one of his self-employed neighbors would visit, wearing his blue apron, and they would both take a moment to go out together and drink a glass of red wine in the nearest bar. The non-conversations that they then carried on at the bar, the snarling back and forth of some sound or other, was what made him feel good. Or else old Gasser would himself go to one of his neighbors, the hairdresser or the tobacconist— having put on his blue apron especially for the purpose—and suggest, on his part, that they go to the bar. The life his father led had made Josef Gasser nervous from the beginning. When, as a child, he would sit around in his father's shop for a couple of hours, helping him do something or other, he had to rush out immediately afterwards and run straight up the nearest hill. Later on, as a schoolboy, he is said to have developed—for some reason or another—certain theories about capitalism and to have immediately started taking an interest in the *Italian economy*. This is what the people of Klausen said after the events. Above all, his former classmates, or his teachers, in particular, suddenly started talking about it all the time, using such general turns of phrase as: Gasser's son always used to talk a lot about the Italian economy, even before he graduated from high school; or: from the beginning, Gasser was always very interested in anything concerning the Italian economy; or: from the beginning, Gasser always looked at the state from the economic point of view, and he knew no area as well as the Italian. Others said that he didn't have the faintest idea about economics and only went on about forms of the economy because, true to the fashion of the day, he wanted to play the communist and so had used the words *Italian economy* simply as an ideological, linguistic weapon; it was nothing but an empty verbal shell, the way such students always use such empty verbal shells. As a pupil, Gasser was always regarded as rebellious, and he later tried to stifle his rebelliousness by reading, for example, books by certain developmental psychologists. For a time he regurgitated general theories (among others Erikson's life-cycle theories) and, for example, talked a lot about *universal statements* and the way in which a young person who does not yet have command of his language develops a feeling of omnipotence by using such universal statements and how this then leads to rebelliousness, since older people, whom he plagues with these statements, know there is nothing beyond a purely grammatical—that is formal—potential backing them up, nothing that has been really experienced and really lived. He regurgitated all this for a time and then threw the books away again and was disgusted with his own theories, which he suddenly regarded as a total pollution of his self. After leaving school, which he finished at seventeen, he went away to the university and did not appear in Klausen again for years. He studied at first in Innsbruck and then later in Berlin. In Berlin, he lost almost all trace of his accent; in fact, on his return hardly a hint of the original could be heard. Journalists maintained that Gasser had never talked much about his time in Berlin, that more could be learned from Sonja Maretsch, who lived with him for a while somewhere in Neu-Kölln. Gasser is said to have lived for a time within the orbit of some left-wing, or radical left-wing, groups and taken part in some activities, all of which were organized by very young people. In retrospect, he is always reported to have called this *the experiment* and always to have spoken very mysteriously about anything to do with it. Soon, it was said, he grew disgusted with the folksy ingratiation of these people or, at least, of certain parts of the factions, who spent their time talking about the importance of social elements, about a just society, *et cetera*. Gasser was thought by then to have gone so far in the renunciation of his concepts that he could no longer envisage what on earth could be meant by the words *just society*. Rumor had it that he increasingly looked upon such concepts as mere linguistic inventions. He is supposed to have said on one occasion: Politicians look for problems to struggle against solely because they are looking for voters, and the best way to appeal to a voter is through the problem that he has, or thinks he has (or that the politician persuades him he has), and that this was all a disgusting process that had never brought anything to people but great duplicity. This and other things were kept ready for use by all classes of society in Klausen in their speculations about Gasser. At the time, Gasser was studying philosophy and sociology and was trying to learn Chinese. He also took acting lessons for a time. When he returned to the Eisack valley he did not go to his parents' house but, for reasons that most people could not fathom, first took a room in the small village of Sankt Leonhard, above Brixen, fifteen kilometers from Klausen. He helped in a sawmill in the neighboring village of Karnol, drove cattle here and there up to pasture, threw dung onto the hillsides, and was always running up to the woods in the direction of Plose, from whence he could look down on Klausen lying very small and peaceful in the valley. The noise of the autobahn was not audible: there were masses of thyme, anemones, and goldcrests up there. Gasser sat at the side of the road, and whenever a BMW from Offenbach, or a Mercedes from Munich, or a party of German motorcyclists drove past him, he watched them with a strange look on his face and chewed the corner of his mouth. A few people saw him sitting up there like this. Now and again he visited Auer in Klausen; Auer was also in Sankt Leonhard once for a few days. Gasser only turned up at his parents after weeks had passed. He left Sankt Leonhard just as suddenly as he had appeared there and moved into the upper part of Klausen. No one could answer the question as to what he had actually been doing in the Eisack valley during these weeks. For a time, it was said that he had been a teacher in Germany, or a social worker. Gasser had neither passed the second qualifying exam as a teacher, nor did he have a diploma for any sort of social work; for most people the latter was, in his case, not even to be imagined. After some time it turned out that, basically, he had been doing nothing. He had worked for a while in an inn in Villanders, then he had helped a farmer build a barn, but these were all short-term activities, nothing that the people of Klausen could call regular breadwinning. If one wished to find a phrase for what the people of Klausen thought Gasser was at that time, it would be *industrious no-good*. Moreover, it was said that, at the time, he gave the impression of being very overbearing: he involved people in conversations that no one wanted to engage in, he deduced that his interlocutors had motives for anything and everything, and he used these conversations to show them up. It was even said that he was able to put someone off the food that was placed before them—people said this with particular reference to the calf's head that he is said to have left untouched in the landlord's, for as we said this abandonment was immediately interpreted politically and almost as an extremist act. Strangely enough, Gasser then actually began some so-called regular work, in fact, in the tourist association. Many people asserted that this work of Gasser's in the tourist association contained a subversive component from the outset. Moreover, it was later maintained that the conversations he had in the various inns had now grown more political and more aggressive. But, as we have said, after what happened, and the more people gossiped, the impression that Gasser left behind in Klausen grew more radical by the day. And what the Klauseners meant by *subversive component* was open to a number of interpretations. There was also a whole number of Klauseners upon whom Gasser—given his circumstances—made a normal impression, though he did seem to them to be somewhat more nervous and quieter than usual, almost reticent, but in no way aggressive. Thus, everything that was said was immediately turned into its opposite with almost legally imposed necessity. Roundabout the time that Gasser is supposed to have been in Feldthurns and the old landlady had supposedly hung up the famous petition in Saint Laurence, he paid his mother one of his rare visits. Later, his sister, Katharina Gasser, also joined them, and as a nervous mood prevailed, people enumerated all the possible things about which a quarrel could break out. Even before Kati's arrival, Gasser was irritable. His mother was sitting on a chair on which, recently, she had always sat, an especially old and shabby chair, which for some reason she had become dotty about. The chair had hardly any cushion left—it was the shabbiest chair in the whole apartment—but she sat on it as though by doing so she wished to demonstrate something, something quite definite, Gasser was sure about this. He himself sat on the couch. He kept looking around, almost compulsively, for he was nervous, although he was not conscious of it. The size of the room made him feel boxed in, and every object in it was too well-known to him. Anyway, everything here was too closely connected with him. When, for example, Gasser looked at his parents' lamp, a misshapen table lamp that had stood on the little table next to the couch for the last twenty-five years, it was as if someone were hitting him on the head with a hammer, and this happened every time he looked at it. What he really wanted to do was to jump up and run out, but he simply sat there and drank tea with his mother. Later on he drank red wine; one glass at first, then another, and finally another, although he had eaten almost nothing that day (he had completely forgotten to). Meanwhile his mother took one magazine after another from the stack on the table and leafed through them. Gasser found this particularly tormenting. At some point he jumped up, started walking round the room, and shouted to her to stop leafing through the magazines, it was driving him crazy. What on earth did she find of interest in them? He took the magazine out of her hand. The Princess of Monaco was featured on the title page! His mother looked at him in astonishment. He: It was none of her business what the Princess of Monaco was doing! Strictly speaking, it wasn't anybody's business! Gasser was almost shouting. All these magazines should be banned, they were disreputable, they were more disreputable than anything in the whole world, they appealed to people's basest instincts, but people did not realize it, people, no they did not realize it. His mother looked at Gasser blankly. But I like to read magazines, she said. For some time now, I've been buying myself one or other of these magazines every now and again. What difference does it make? They're just magazines. Gasser: No, they are not just magazines. There was no such thing as *just*. Nothing was *just*, and it was especially true of these magazines. She: I don't know what you suddenly have against these magazines. Your friend Paolucci works for a magazine like this, and you have nothing against that. Gasser: Paolucci works for a political magazine, that is something different, that is something quite different, and, incidentally, Paolucci was not his friend. He had nothing to do with him. What do you mean you have nothing to do with him? Georg Paolucci was such a nice boy and very helpful. He had even been shopping for her the other day. He had also bought this magazine for her. You don't go shopping for me. Gasser stood still. What did she mean, Paolucci went shopping for her? She didn't even know him. She: He was here recently looking for you for something or other, he also told me that you had often seen each other lately in the Cellar, and then he offered to help me, I have so much trouble with my legs. He: What did he want from me? And why was he looking for me here? I don't live with you, he knows that well enough. Perhaps he wanted to see Kati . . . yes, that could be possible, of course, he wanted to see Kati . . . as for the rest, she was right. There is no difference between her magazines and Paolucci's periodical; they're all the same. You go soft in the head, you forget everything at once, and above all you forget the truth, that's the law of the world. She: She didn't understand a word of what he was talking about. What law was he talking about? Oh dear, she understood him less and less. He had become such a stranger to her. Gasser rolled his eyes. She: She liked to read the magazines because she always found something about Kati in them nowadays. He: That's what I thought. But can you explain why you read these reports about Kati? It is, after all, just a lot of rubbish. Why did she read the reports? She: Why did she read the reports? After all, they concerned her daughter. She wanted to find out what was being written about her daughter, that was her prerogative. He: It's got nothing to do with prerogative. What does it have to do with prerogative? But how are you to understand that? . . . So, it makes you happy, reading these articles about your daughter? But these articles have nothing whatsoever to do with your daughter, for they all function according to the same pattern, Kati only serves to illustrate these ideas, don't you understand? The ideas are always the same. They have nothing to do with Kati. Everything is interchangeable. It is all interchangeable, but that is something you don't understand. She: She did not understand that, no. There was only one thing she did understand: recently, all he wanted to do was ruin everything for her. Anything that gave her pleasure, he destroyed. He had really developed a special ability to do that, to spoil everything for her. But she couldn't allow herself to be tormented like this, by everything. As she said this, Gasser once more rolled his eyes. After a while: A lot of people even collect these articles about Kati; did you know for example that Anton Kerschbaumer, who lives in the upper part of town, possesses every article that has been written about her? Wherever a picture of her is to be seen, he cuts it out; Kati has herself photographed at the Kälterer. See, you know, the photograph with the bath towel, she was in one of these illustrated magazines . . . some such paper . . . and Kerschbaumer cuts it out. He even has it pinned up over his washbasin. Kati in a bath towel, I've seen it there myself. Look at it sometime—like that! Can't you see what we are talking about? She: She did not know . . . they were, after all, only articles. Kati is a pretty girl. She is successful. That's nice. At this, Gasser nearly had a tantrum. It made him furious when his mother used expressions like "but that is nice" or even "but that is quite natural" or even "that is quite normal." Meanwhile he had given up explaining to her that these expressions had no substance, they meant absolutely nothing. Gasser thought that people should never have been allowed to get their hands on words like nice, natural, and normal, because they, the people, used them to justify everything; they even used expressions like "but that is nice" to justify the ultimate absurdity. Gasser bit his lips. His mother: And one day you will accomplish something, I am absolutely certain of that. What am I going to accomplish? asked Gasser, now completely dumbfounded. She: Of course you will accomplish something! You are still so young, you are clever, you still have something ahead of you, I know you have. Kati became an actress, you mustn't be jealous of that; because everyone becomes what they are, and what they are capable of, and your abilities simply lie elsewhere. Gasser looked at his mother. She suddenly seemed more and more strange to him. What do you mean by that? he asked. I'm not jealous of Kati, where do you get that idea? And, anyway, what are these abilities that I'm supposed to have? She: Well . . . the abilities . . . just something you're interested in . . . For instance, you used to draw ever so nicely. I still have so many of your drawings. You used to draw pine-trees and ships, sailing ships. He: You must be crazy. She: He shouldn't talk to his mother like that! His mother was not crazy. No, he had a talent for drawing, she knew that. By the way, she'd found out that he'd taken up drawing again in the meantime. That made her very happy (as she said this, Gasser's mother looked very happy, apparently just because her son was drawing again). Gasser asked incredulously what all of this was supposed to mean, what was he drawing? He wasn't doing any drawing at all. How did she get that idea? She: But Perluttner saw you recently. You were sitting down by the church and had a pad on your knees, and on it you were drawing something you had observed down there. You always were a sort of observer, you observe everything, very precisely and exactly. Now Gasser laughed, for he remembered the incident. He really had been sitting down there, but for quite different reasons than his mother assumed. Admittedly he said nothing about what the reasons were . . . he would never have talked to his mother about the reasons, he spoke to practically nobody about the reasons, indeed he had not thought that anyone had paid any attention to his sitting down by the church making a sketch, for he really had sat there and sketched something, something very definite . . . And what did I draw, he asked gloomily, did Perluttner see that too? She: No. When he spoke to you, you immediately closed the pad. That's what you always did when you were a child. You didn't want anyone to see what you were drawing. (Again, thought

Gasser, she has this strange enthusiastic look. Always when she talks about my childhood. When I was younger I always shut my pad up if anyone watched me while I was drawing, aha, that sparks her enthusiasm, this nonsense warms her heart.) Gasser jumped up again and paced from one end of the room to the other faster and faster. Even when his sister came into the room, he kept on pacing up and down in the same way; he scarcely greeted Kati, just gave a slight wave of the hand. Kati kissed her mother and sat down on the couch. She was talking about something, Gasser only heard fragments. (He had noticed recently that he was only aware of everything or, at least most things, in fragments, because his thoughts were always distracted by something else. Certainly whatever he became aware of greeted him with a nagging excess of clarity.) She was saying that she had a few days break from shooting; she was living in the Goldener Elefant. Of course she had been constantly accosted, on the street outside; she had been nothing short of hounded, they had pursued her right up to the front door . . . Gasser looked down into the street. It was true, a bunch of people were standing there and pointing up at the windows of the Gassers' apartment: Kerschbaum was there, Moreth the alderman, the old Gruber woman—a group of some Klauseners who, ever since her arrival, had pursued his sister through the streets, hunting for an autograph from, or a scrap of conversation with, this Klausener woman who had recently become famous. There, look at alderman Moreth with his red face, so he's one of them, Gasser said to himself . . . Hardly does someone from the TV come into the town than these Klauseners immediately regress several stages in their development . . . He looked at the cluster of people for quite a while; they were now breaking up, and after a few minutes the street was again empty. Gasser kept on laughing, while he continued staring out of the window, murmuring something to himself that his mother and his sister could not catch. He seemed to be completely out of it as he stood staring at the empty street. What is there to laugh about? asked his mother. He: What do you mean, laughing? Was I laughing? Oh yes, now I remember, I did just laugh, I was laughing at Alderman Moreth. His sister from the couch: How did he hit upon Alderman Moreth? And why was he so terribly nervous all the time? Gasser: I hit upon Alderman Moreth because he was quoted in the *Tagblatt* today. Everything Moreth said there sounded so sensible; incidentally, he was talking about the civic initiative that Taschner had proposed, but I'm sure you know nothing about that, you've not been here in Klausen for quite a while . . . Now, at least, what Moreth says sounds so sensible when it appears in the newspaper, but when you see him in front of you, as a person, with his red head, and with such strange desires . . . people as a whole have such strange desires when they are in private and, presumably, he was in private down there. What desires was he talking about? asked Kati. It must have been some sort of desires said Gasser, otherwise he would not have followed you through half the upper town. Kati said she did not know this Moreth person at all, what was he talking about all this time? Gasser laughed and clapped his hands enthusiastically . . . for a while all three of them said nothing; Gasser was looking very thoughtful again. He was still standing in front of the narrow window and was looking at the now empty street, as though something still held his attention down there. Then: Our mother has lately suggested that I am jealous of you. Oh, yes! I am jealous of you, I admit it. But do you also know what I am jealous of? She: No. My God he's got to stop thinking all these things, it does him no good. He just makes himself unhappy. Why on earth does he always torment himself about everything? He: I envy you because everything is so egregiously easy for you. You do what you do, that's why I envy you. You didn't even exert yourself to enter your profession, I know that, even if everyone now says it was different and maintains that the movies were always your one goal in life (because that's what you've been maintaining lately in all the magazines). And although you didn't exert yourself to enter your profession and everything happened more or less easily; you never had any sort of goal, you evidently felt no need for one in the process—you simply accept it all the same and are satisfied. She: But yes, why should she not be satisfied? Gasser started walking restlessly up and down again. He knew that what he said could not be understood . . . Then he stopped and stared at his mother and sister. He lapsed deeper and deeper into strange thoughts; I'm a completely normal person, he said. I work in the tourist association, I'm someone like everyone else. I'd like you both to be aware of that. Gasser clapped his hands, looked quite euphoric and shouted: Yes, exactly, now you have it! I'm like everyone else! It was actually a mistake to go to the university and leave here, you were right from the beginning. There is nothing to say about me, mark my words. That is what is most important: that there is nothing to say about a person. It is, in some nauseating way, all imaginary. I can't stand it. And that is the truth, the only truth. Do you understand? That everything is the same and the differences are based entirely on vanity. His mother said that she did not understand a single word. She did not even know what he was talking about these days. Of course he was the same as everybody else, how could it be otherwise, what sort of a strange idea was that? And why was he talking about the truth, how did he suddenly arrive at truth? He had grown so strange. Gasser clenched his fists. Then he contorted his face in an ugly fashion, for he thought he couldn't stand it any longer and simply had to leave. He was now standing in the doorway looking at his mother and was considering the following: Why does she continually sit on that chair? She had started sitting on this chair, quite ostentatiously, a little while ago. Look here, that's what she's saying, here's this old shabby chair, it really is very shabby, it's already in tatters, and I sit down on it. I, not you. The oldest and shabbiest chair, and it's just right for me, for I sit down on it and that's exactly where I belong, that's my place in the world and that is my one real act vis-à-vis the world, namely to sit down on this chair, otherwise there's nothing in which I have the slightest interest . . . Gasser now suddenly felt like pulling his mother off the chair and screaming in her face and telling her that she should finally stop belittling herself in this ostentatious and, above all, vain manner, he'd seen through her, she was doing it all simply for reasons of vanity . . . this whole ostentatious reduction was making him almost boil over with rage . . . but he didn't say a word, just took his coat and left. It wasn't until he was downstairs and out in the street that he very slowly pulled himself together. He simply walked along the road for a bit and did not even notice where he was walking. He looked very strange now, for his eyes were staring into the distance in an odd manner. Too annoying, he said to himself. Why on earth did I go there in the first place? They understand nothing, and I, likewise, cannot understand them—they are complete strangers to me. He stopped and had a feeling that he must take a deep breath. Then he once again lapsed into thought: So, your sister has simply become the actress Kati Gasser. That's how it is, for no reason. And she is getting married and is even talking about a desire to have children . . . Yes, really: and, of all things, she is going to marry this Martin Delazer. Now, it comes back to me: Among other things, the reason why I wanted to get together with her was, at all costs, to talk her out of marrying this Martin Delazer. That's really what's most important: namely, that she should not marry this Martin Delazer. But I forgot; I don't think I even touched on the subject. How on earth did she come up with this person? They're staging it for the magazines, I know it, but she won't admit it. "The Dream Wedding of the South Tyrol" is what they'll call it in the magazines. The famous actress, the famous architect, you can see it in front of you already. That's how she'll plunge into calamity. But wait, it's possible she won't even notice that for her it is a calamity. For that's the way it is; almost everyone plunges into calamity, they plunge themselves and the others with them into calamity, and don't notice it and simply think it's their happiness or, at the very least, something completely normal, so normal that they don't notice anything about it. No, she should marry Paolucci. Paolucci grows nervous when the conversation turns to my sister, that's obvious, but he says nothing about it. But why am I thinking about Paolucci now? . . . She wants to have children with Delazer because they will be her happiness, the Delazer-Gasser children. What an ideology! A totally theoretical ideology, a wish for children like that. I cannot think of anything more theoretical. In the old days, I often used to think that childbearing is a completely theoretical-ideological act that had nothing to do with Nature, but then I forgot that thought, because it is really very odd. But when I see Kati now, the total unnaturalness in her face, the strange ring of her words, the whole artificiality of these people . . . of almost all people . . . Now I think that thought again. I cannot do anything else; I have to think that way because it really is the truth about Kati, and when the truth forces itself upon me, I cannot dismiss it from my thoughts, no matter how strange it might sound. I have to think it and not dismiss it from my thoughts when it forces itself on me. That is the truth. And my mother has no idea about anything and thinks and acts only in terms of belittling herself, and that is why she sits down on that chair. I think she even carried it down from the attic herself, just so that she could sit down on it again. She wishes to be nothing, she wants to be nothing at all, and the fact is she wants to be nothing ostentatiously, fully conscious of what she is doing, and that is really absurd. But, your father Gasser, yes, your father . . . he at least is a somebody! A somebody because he does not produce any words. He is totally out of it, your father, and, for that reason, he is a somebody. He wants nothing (and he doesn't even know that he wants nothing), and he says nothing. That is the highest level a person can reach, you cannot reach a higher one . . . Earlier on, I used to be contemptuous of my father because of that; today I can no longer be. Incidentally, he rides a bicycle. His whole life is arranged so that he can bicycle nine hundred meters, twice a day. One of these days, people will understand that that is not unimportant, that perhaps that is the most important thing of all, those nine hundred meters on his bicycle; anyway, no one will be able to express it so that it would be understood. Yes, they should erect a statue to my father. Those nine hundred meters . . . those nine hundred meters . . . At that moment all these strange and confused thoughts appeared completely lucid to Gasser. Meanwhile, he had stopped for a moment and recollected that he had actually wanted to go to the Cellar. He wanted to meet Auer there because of a letter he had been carrying with him in his coat all this while; he had also forgotten the letter the whole time, even though it was possible that the letter was very important to Auer. But there was something else besides . . . namely that he now suddenly had the feeling, up here by Nussbaumer's, that someone was watching him. The feeling was familiar to him; for some time now he had repeatedly had the feeling that someone was standing behind him, watching him. Recently everyone had been wanting something from him; a lot of people approached him, either asking about his famous sister, or wanting to know something about his days in Berlin, and he was frequently quite directly approached about certain ideas that people said they had heard something about. Gasser was surprised at how easily one could become the Klauseners' center of attention. He turned around, for he was very eager to learn who was standing behind him and watching him. It was Paolucci. Gasser eyed the other Klausener from head to foot . . . Perhaps Paolucci had been standing there for some time, observing him; that could well be. Perhaps, thought Gasser, I just started thinking about Paolucci because he's been standing round here the whole time. How strange it all is. As though everything was taken out of context a short time ago . . . all causalities. I'm walking around out here, Paolucci is standing here, here in the upper part of Klausen. Everything could be . . . everything connected with this thought, every word could be replaced by another, and yet everything would remain exactly the same, even if that perhaps appears very strange. And yet to me it all appears lucid and logical, more lucid and more logical than anything else. I should call upon him to marry my sister; yes, really, I would be only too glad to present the idea to him seriously . . . Gasser looked at his former classmate. In the past few days Paolucci had been looking like an Italian; he seemed to be cultivating it. He let his black hair grow long and had grown a full beard. And he was getting fatter and fatter; he had grown really obese while Gasser was in Berlin. Paolucci went to Milan a lot these days and was trying to gain a foothold in a newspaper there. For weeks he had been following a case, a lawsuit, the case of Laner, that had been brought to the public's attention in the South Tyrolean press; a case in which Delazer, Kati's fiancé, was also somehow involved. And, Gasser asked, had he reached Laner in the meantime? He had said he wanted to reach him, at least, if he remembered correctly, he had told him yesterday that he did. No, there was no reaching Laner any more, said Paolucci. He had spoken to him on the phone the day before yesterday, but since then he had isolated himself. If you called him at home, his wife would answer. She always said that Laner was not at home. Gasser: Aha. Gasser went on listening, but with a certain impatience, not really interested in what the other Klausener was saying. It had all been in the newspaper a thousand times, said Paolucci, and I also saw him on Italian TV recently playing the innocent victim of the legal system. I do not understand why people like Laner don't have to spend even three weeks in jail. Not even three weeks. He was sentenced to eighteen months, but after three weeks of judicial investigation he's out again. And what all do we hear now! His wife and his brother, we are told, stood by him all the time, the whole arduous three weeks. People are still sorry for them! As recently as yesterday, when I was here at Nussbaumer's, I heard people talking about Laner. It was sinful, they said, what had happened to the poor man and his family. It was a concession to the Reds they said; it had been a political trial they said. That's how they talk about Laner; Laner's one of us after all. When the trial was on, you could hear people saying this wherever you went, in the whole Eisack valley. Laner's one of us, he's always been one of us, they say, and his whole trial is taking place for no reason, no reason at all. Gasser shifted from one foot to the other; he could not understand Paolucci's interest in the whole thing—in fact he couldn't understand him at all. He only had one memory, one memory of a very specific form of thinking that Paolucci obviously still practiced, in spite of the fact that, in Gasser's view, this form of thinking was bound to crumble into dust in one's hands. Yes, that's South Tyrol, said Paolucci. (He seemed almost enthusiastic). Our country is a little tiny flea pit of a theater; of course the world sees nothing of it. Beneath this cloak the South Tyroleans can do whatever they like. Everything here is so obviously matted together that it is impossible to make a stranger understand how perfectly open everything is. Everybody sees it, everyone keeps their mouth shut, they all consent. But, you know, when ninety-five percent of the South Tyroleans are satisfied with everything as it is and approve of it (for they do approve of things as they are; that they should be different would seem impossible to them), then you have to come to terms with it. That's democracy. After all, you cannot run around with a machine gun shouting, "Right! All the idiots on the left and all the others on the right." Certain questions would be asked at once: What exactly was meant by idiot, and what were the criteria for it, and how did it come about that you yourself possessed the criteria? . . . and so on. Who then is this you yourself, actually? asked Gasser. He had, in reality, stopped listening and was, in a strange way, stuck thinking about who the people themselves were, of whom Paolucci had been speaking. What exactly had Paolucci been talking about? Had he used the word machine gun? What a strange coincidence, thought Gasser, that Paolucci should start talking about a machine gun; there was no obvious connection, and so it had to be regarded as a strange coincidence. What did you want to know about Laner? Gasser then asked, picking up the thread of the earlier conversation again. Paolucci was rumored to have been on the track of the story for some weeks; he, Gasser, had at the beginning been completely unable to understand what the Milanese journalist had found so fascinating about the Laner case. Well, said Paolucci, what did he want to ask him? . . . First of all, he wanted to ask him about the circumstances of his arrest. Herr Laner, under arrest for three weeks, how does one envisage something like that? *Et cetera*. Gasser: It wasn't three weeks. It was two weeks and five days. Paolucci: Of course he would have come to that. But first he would have asked him a couple of innocuous questions; for example: Herr Laner, did you receive any letters in jail? Herr Laner, would you tell our readers the contents of those letters? Herr Laner, did you take notice of the readers' opinions about your case that appeared in the daily papers? He would have asked questions like that at first, then he would have asked him questions which would have hemmed him in more and more as he proceeded from question to question . . . After that he would have asked him about the moral evaluation of his, Laner's, business dealings in the Sarn valley, and he would have confronted him with the fact that even the governor had admitted that it was necessary to investigate whether or not Agriculture Minister Laner had willfully refused to take into account the damage which his undertakings would wreak on consumers and on the countryside. Gasser was now laughing almost morbidly. The governor would never leave Laner in the lurch! he shouted, never, it was completely unthinkable. How on earth did Paolucci get such an absurd idea? Besides, it was totally unimportant, the whole matter was absolutely unimportant. That was what he had been trying to tell him the whole time, namely how completely unimportant and superfluous this, and especially his, Paolucci's, detailed way of looking at things was. Whether the following had never occurred to him: If it had not been Laner who had destroyed half the Sarn valley with his projects, then it would simply have been someone else, and if it hadn't been the Sarn valley, then it would have simply been some other valley, because they all did the same thing at the same time, and if one of them dropped out, another would immediately step in and take his place, that was human law. Paolucci: Of late he was always talking about human law, what was that supposed to mean? He, Paolucci, knew of no such law. What did he mean by it? Well, said Gasser, looking past Paolucci in a very strange manner at the wall of the house opposite . . . Paolucci once again emphasized that he had been very well prepared for the interview; he had also heard from a few elected members of the People's Party, who were absolutely supportive of the magazine and its approach. The whole case had to be retried. Some thought this would be the greatest legal scandal in South Tyrol since the Comploi case. They continued talking for a while about Gasser's sister. Gasser said that Delazer and Kati had submitted a prenuptial agreement to the attorney Trombini. He said that both parties had been negotiating the agreement for a few weeks. A lot of money was involved. Delazer was a tough negotiator. Admittedly, his sister was too. Trombini had first taken the view that it was really unusual for Klauseners to draw up such an agreement. But then when the facts were presented to him, that is to say the incomes . . . he, Paolucci, must consider—in Kati's case . . . Milan, Rome, the large studios . . . in Delazer's case, Bolzano, the South Tyrolean state parliament, the many magazines, the projects, all the money . . . and of course Trombini is earning his *lire* in the process. It must be Klausen's richest marriage ever. Indeed, said Paolucci, looking at the wall opposite with as expressionless a face as possible. The subject was obviously not one that he liked. And when, Gasser asked, did you last speak to my sister? Paolucci: That must have been about six months ago. She has such a lot to do, he said, why should she bother about us Klauseners? Besides, he did not move in the same world as Kati did. Gasser: But why not? That was no obstacle. Kati happened to be in Klausen for a few days, and if Paolucci liked, he could arrange a meeting. Paolucci: But why? There was absolutely no reason why he should. He had nothing to do with his sister. Gasser: But he really hadn't meant that Paolucci should write about his sister. Paolucci: And what had he meant? Gasser: He hadn't meant anything. Paolucci: It would of course be very interesting to talk to her about Delazer. At the moment Delazer was keeping very much in the background, but it won't always be like that. He, Paolucci, was convinced that Delazer was playing a justifiable part in Laner's case. But in all honesty, he didn't want to burden Kati with something of this sort . . . she really had much too much to do. She's as good as never in Klausen any longer, she's bought herself an apartment in Rome, I've heard. Gasser: Where did you hear that from? People keep telling me that Kati has bought an apartment in Rome, but that is simply not true. Where does that come from? Paolucci said he thought that he had read it somewhere. You mean in one of the magazines? Paolucci: I don't know. Perhaps someone else had read it and had then told him; he had no idea, anyway it wasn't so important. After that, Gasser left Paolucci behind in the street and walked on, but not to the Cellar. His thoughts now grew darker and darker, and he also suddenly felt an urgent need to take a lot of deep breaths. Josef Gasser was really in a very strange condition. Had anyone seen him they would have thought he was ill, as though he had a fever . . . but he was often like that these days, though he did not know what to do about it . . . the attacks kept on recurring, and yet each time they seemed to be new and final . . . the house walls, the eternally monotonous bay windows, that all seemed to be about to collapse on top of him . . . Why, he thought, now almost aggressively, have we South Tyroleans always built bay windows on our houses? Wherever there's a house, there's a bay window on it. And anyway, why did we build these streets so narrow? For ever and ever, so narrow, as though the South Tyroleans had from the very beginning only one thing in mind: namely, to build streets that were as narrow as possible. And they all stand behind their bay windows and look out on the street, all in the same way. Just as, previously, I also was standing at the window, the bay window, in my mother's house, looking out at the street. You stand there like a porcelain figure . . . No! Away. I must get away from here at once! Gasser ran up the stone steps to Säben, and the higher up the steps he ran, the more liberated he felt. In the meantime, he had reached Castle Branzoll and was sitting on a bench and looking across the valley to the other side, to the chain of mountains, the forests, the railroad station, the autobahn and was chewing the corners of his mouth. He sat there for quite a while . . . Later on, incidentally, two people, at least, maintained that they had seen him up there: Hanspaul Meraner, who lived in the Färbergasse, and Giuseppe Neri, an Italian retiree who lived in the Oberweg; both of them later expatiated in various places, above all at Nussbaumer's and the Bolzano police station, on Gasser and his progress up to Branzoll . . . Meraner, a gardener up at Branzoll, related for his part that the whole time he was up there Gasser was restlessly walking up and down with a strangely contorted expression, and suddenly he went up to an alder tree and looked at it in a way that was stranger than he, Hanspaul Meraner, had ever seen in his whole life. Gasser, he said, had looked at the alder very attentively for at least ten minutes, as though something very decisive depended on it. However, in Meraner's other versions the tree in question was suddenly a beech and, later on, a spruce. Gasser reportedly walked up and down in front of the tree, then suddenly stopped, stamped on the ground several times, and slapped his thigh like a Rumpelstiltskin (according to Meraner, Gasser was in a very unusual mood). Later, Meraner said, he sat down on a bench and suddenly took some papers out of his pocket, on which he began making some notes or sketches, looking across the valley, that is towards the east, all the time. (At the time many people said that Gasser had made notes or sketches in the most diverse places). In any case, Gasser had always been looking towards the east, very intensively, almost compulsively, although there was nothing there except for the mountain opposite and the autobahn viaduct in front of it. Later on Gasser is said to have looked very satisfied and to have disappeared again. Meraner could see everything exactly as it happened from the garden in which he had just been cutting roses, *et cetera*. Neri reported something quite different. For one thing (and this was very important to him), the Italian stated that Meraner had not been in the garden at Branzoll; Meraner had certainly not seen Gasser up there, or he had concocted it all subsequently, either because he was drunk or because, out of braggadocio, he wanted to tell the newspapers something about Gasser even though he had nothing to tell. Possibly, Neri hinted, the owner of Branzoll, a member of the minor nobility from Piedmont, had instructed Meraner to tell such stories about Gasser, to dispel certain suspicions, with which she herself had been confronted during the investigation. Neri, who suffered from nagging arthritis and was therefore forced to take long walks, wanted to take a walk up there on the day in question. He claimed to have seen Gasser up in Branzoll, not however on a bench or in front of an alder or a spruce, but sitting in the garden itself, on a stone bench between two pots of oleanders. His facial expression revealed that he was in the very best of moods; he kept on looking up at the room with a balcony that was next to the tower, and he had seemed lively and in high spirits. After a while the owner had appeared, and nothing suggested that she was surprised to see Gasser sitting there in her garden. At least she had neither waved nor reacted in any other way. On the contrary, she had immediately disappeared again. Gasser had apparently taken no notice of anything that was going on. However, as though on a prearranged, but for Neri invisible, signal, Gasser had suddenly gone into the castle, straight through the main entrance, which was obviously unlocked. After this, Neri had—with great pain, but even greater curiosity—sat for a solid hour on a bench until, he said, Gasser came out again through the main entrance. Neri could not swear to this (this is what he told the Bolzano police), but Gasser had made a much changed impression on him: his hair and his clothes were in disorder. It could also be seen that Gasser now made a thoughtful impression and that he was carrying a parcel under his arm—a very dubious and puzzling, rather long, parcel, like the one that was later found on the other side of the Eisack not far from the lime silo. Gasser's parcel is supposed to have looked very like the parcel by the lime silo; indeed it was said to be identical with it. He, Neri, said he actually believed that there were red and black letters on the parcel, just as there were on the one that was found not far from the lime silo and which had been pictured in the *Alto Adige*. Gasser was said to have walked some ten meters from the castle, then suddenly to have looked at the parcel enthusiastically, even lovingly, and to have turned it over in his hands extremely carefully. Then to have sat down upon a stone, opened the parcel, and taken certain things out of it . . . at this point, however, Neri's detailed memories suddenly dried up. For now he always spoke only of objects (*cose*) and possibly technical devices (*apparecchi*), all of which he was unable to recognize, as he had had to keep himself in the background and look at everything from a distance, for it is true that this and that about Gasser had even then slipped away from him, *et cetera*. Hanspaul Meraner, for his part, rejected the whole of Neri's story as total nonsense. Of course, rumors arose later on of a relationship between Gasser and the woman who owned the castle, and, as far as that went, those who believed there was a liaison were counterbalanced by those who said that Gasser did not know the woman at all. Because of this, the aforementioned Piedmontese woman was soon exposed to a certain amount of gossip in the valley. This was, naturally, only because she lived up in the castle alone with her two children. A single woman, a castle, the seclusion, the lemon trees on the terrace, the oleander, wealth, it was inevitable that people would start talking about every car that drove up there and begin making up stories. Gasser already stood accused of dubious relationships in other places. That seemed to arise out of sheer necessity: Whenever people start gossiping about someone, stories about some sort of lechery spring up around him, like weeds, emanating from fully adult people who are not remarkable for anything else. (Gasser was even accused by certain people of having peddled revealing pictures of his sister, although such pictures were never discovered.) It was also not impossible that innumerable versions of the parcel story were circulated later, in every possible place, and the allegation that persisted most obstinately was that the parcel contained a special rifle with telescopic sights for long-distance shots. The less people were able to say about where the rumor originated (that is, who originated it) the more precise it became. Several makes of rifle were mentioned by Klauseners who were familiar with rifles, until finally there was only one. With this rifle, it was said, it was easily possible to shoot someone through the heart at a distance of five hundred meters, even when visibility was poor or it was very dark. Until their withdrawal from service, these rifles had been used by special units of the East German army. Gasser's rifle came from these unwanted stocks. Gasser was supposed to have learned to use the rifles in Berlin, in the left wing cells to which he belonged, *et cetera*. Up there, sitting on the stone, Gasser had presumably, people said, assembled the special rifle as a trial, checked it out and apparently fired a few pretend shots across to the other side of the Eisack, because the rifle had been acquired by him and his group to bridge the distance, from one bank of the Eisack to the other. It was said at Nussbaumer's that if Neri had not perceived all this, it was only because all the Italians here were slow-witted, completely unworldly, idiots. Giuseppe Neri is also very short-sighted. And, of course, he only made his statement after the photograph of the rather long parcel that was found beside the lime silo had been seen in the newspaper. Gasser walked through Klausen an hour later—after Neri is supposed to have seen all of this—not, incidentally, carrying a parcel. He went into the Cellar at about seven o'clock. A few people—including Hanspaul Meraner and his wife—were sitting at tables with white tablecloths and eating dinner in the front room. Meraner greeted Gasser quite inconspicuously. His wife, however, stopped Gasser and bombarded him with various questions about his sister and X, the famous actor. Frau Meraner asked whether Kati Gasser really had a relationship with X? But, Maria, said Meraner, that's really none of our business. Why is it none of our business? I'm interested in it. X had always interested her, she said. (To Gasser): I watch every program that X is in. He was recently in . . . that was nice (Frau Meraner mentioned an Austrian TV program). He was cooking in it. Roulades, I think, beef roulades. Herr Meraner: What are you telling Josef that for? She: If his sister didn't have a relationship with X, why should she kiss him this evening? It was so strange, everyone here is amazed; suddenly she kisses him! And she had gotten engaged only a few weeks ago. Meraner: People are constantly kissing on the television. Everyone kisses everyone else, that's not reality, that has nothing to do with her engagement, what are you talking about? She: But she never kissed him before! He suddenly dies, and she kisses him. Quite suddenly. She never kissed him before. Twenty-five episodes without a kiss. Well take a look at the episode first, said Meraner. He drew his wife back to the table. Gasser went on through the restaurant into the actual cellar. The back, and lower, room of the restaurant is an old vault where there are tables made out of barrels; there are also a few larger barrels where three or four people can sit. It was fairly smoky; Gasser saw Auer sitting alone at a table. Sonja was sitting with Hans Moreth, the son of the alderman, at another table. At a table a bit further away sat Pareith, the painter, the one whose old-style oil painting—*A View of the Town of Klausen*—was sold, all over the place, as a postcard to tourists; Gasser, too, sold it almost daily in the tourist agency. Otherwise there was no one else in the room. Gasser shut the heavy iron door behind him. The room was decorated in dark earth-toned colors, a lot of wood, old tools on the walls. Little lamps were alight above those present, so that their faces appeared in cones of light. Sonja and Moreth looked at Gasser when he came in. Pareith sat there smoking a cigar, a cheroot, and was saying something or other. Gasser did not immediately grasp the situation. It seemed to him that Pareith was talking to Auer all the time. Pareith was, as always, talking about art, although he was not actually an artist, more a craftsman. Nevertheless, he always talked about art, painting, but also about philosophy. Auer was not responding to him in any way. He sat there alone, in his cone of light, with a glass of red wine, staring intently at the grain of his wooden tabletop and not moving. When Sonja said something, clearly to take the burden off Auer, Pareith immediately answered that *what she said was very interesting, of course it was important to consider something else in the matter, and that was such and such*. Gasser sat down next to Sonja, and the landlord came in and brought him a glass of wine. And do you know, said Pareith, who had now turned back to Auer, that's why I like coming here so much. These colors! Yes, these heavy dark colors. They're like my pictures. I always paint in these colors. You have to find yourself in art. You have to work hard, and when you have found yourself you must stay with yourself . . . that is, of course you have to keep renewing yourself, said Pareith, who drew on his cigar, leaned back, gave a sweeping look around the room, and then blew the smoke out again. In my opinion, said Moreth, all this paraphernalia should be taken off the walls again. Why are all these harrows and wagon wheels hanging up here? The landlord hung all this stuff up five years ago; it bothered me from the beginning. This is a cellar-vault, not a barn. And the landlord was, of course, never a farmer. Moreth shook his head. First and foremost, one should always consider one's own artistic achievements, said Pareith, one's own artistic aspirations and the result. As an artist—he, Pareith, had always seen it that way—one should always aspire to really great things, one should always have the highest aspirations in mind, and one should never lose sight of them. (At this point he raised his index finger). Art, yes art, is always the balance between the most extreme poles. The greatest balance is always found in the greatest art. Take painting for example. You can study it all in my picture, *A View of the Town of Klausen*. The manner in which the axes run together, the way the brown at the top, below the monastery, is caught up by the white spray of the Eisack. He had, he said, worked a long time to achieve that. (Leaning back): Anyway, the picture was accepted. It became a famous picture. But, of course, self-praise is no recommendation. Auer had been sitting there restlessly the whole time saying nothing, but now he did say something. He said, this picture is the only picture that Pareith ever sold successfully, he would never again sell one for so much money, he would sell his pictures, as he did previously, to idiots for the cheapest prices, for bars and lounges and so on. Pareith leaned back indignantly. Now listen, he said. Auer: And he could tell him exactly why he had been successful with *A View of the Town of Klausen*. Pareith: He had been successful with *A View of the Town of Klausen* because it is a good picture and a profound work. People see that at once, they can see when they are dealing with a clean and profound work. Auer grinned and went on looking at the grain of his table-top. Oh! come on, he said. Pareith: Well, what other reasons are there for the picture to have been a success? The picture is a success simply for its own sake . . . Auer looked at Gasser. Tell him, he said. I, why me? asked Gasser. Auer: After all, it's hanging in your office on the wall as a poster, you see it every day, you sell the posters to tourists, so you tell him. Pareith looked expectantly at Gasser. The question now really seemed to torment him: why had his picture been accepted by the city if not for reasons of its quality? They bought it of course and value it so highly because . . . Pareith: Yes, yes, because . . . ? Pareith was scarcely able to wait for the answer any longer, he was completely keyed up. Gasser: The city simply and solely bought the picture because you left out the autobahn. Pareith: I beg your pardon? What did that have to do with it? Left out the autobahn? He didn't understand. Gasser: And the Eisack valley road is also missing. Pareith: But why should he have painted the Eisack valley road? He wanted to paint Klausen for heaven's sake, not the Eisack valley road. Auer: And the bacon factory is missing, the limestone works as well, to say nothing of the dam at the reservoir—that, of course, is not there either. Besides all of this, he had painted the Eisack with a green bank. Pareith stared at him, aghast. He did not understand a word. What did they have against a green bank? Auer and Sonja started to smirk at each other. They started laughing at this and that detail of *A View of the Town of Klausen* and said to Pareith that all the intelligentsia of the Eisack valley laughed their heads off at the picture; of course all the other towns envied Klausen this picture, it was worth its weight in gold. Auer: Pareith has simply omitted their old school's gymnasium and replaced it with a few apple trees (in full bloom, of course). But, my dear people, said Pareith, that's all for an artistic reason. Auer: There's an artistic reason for everything in your eyes. Pareith: And of course the reason is that, from the angle I chose, the gymnasium would loom up much too high in the foreground. It would be much too dominant, the gymnasium. Trees are better there, you can see that in the end result . . . Even Moreth slapped his thighs with laughter and exclaimed that Pareith even begrudged the Klausen children their gymnasium, that was curious . . . to be sure he had not noticed that before, he really must look at the picture more closely. Auer: So that's the reason why this enormous painting was accepted, because your picture has as much to do with Klausen as bacon from the bacon factory has to do with South Tyrolean bacon, namely, absolutely nothing—but it does sell well. Pareith stood up and walked around; he now considered everyone present in the room envious. He even asserted that he was a patriot; he loved his town, and the reason he had painted the picture the way he did was that this was the true Klausen, the Klausen of his heart, but after a while he composed himself, sat down in his place again with a new cigar between his stubby fingers, and started anew to talk about art and the great expectations people had of it. After a while, some more people came in—among others, a German man in his mid-fifties and a slender athletic Italian, who was perhaps twenty years younger than

the German. Paolucci also put in an appearance. The German and
the Italian were having a discussion: the younger man was explaining
something to the older one; the latter appeared demoralized, rubbed
his temples several times, and looked helplessly at his younger inter-
locutor. Both of them were talking Italian and German. The young
man, evidently a Florentine, was aiming a barrage of words at the
older one; Gasser could not at first establish a context, but he kept
hearing words like maxims and parameter; they were talking on the
whole in a scholarly jargon, and the young man slapped the other
one on the shoulders several times, at which the latter slumped down
even more and seemed almost more demoralized. Gasser did not
know either of them. Pareith got up and went over to the German
and shook his hand. Herr Professor Klein, he said, it is a pleasure to
see you. Please join in a little conversation about art, we were just
saying that . . . He broke off abruptly when he noticed that the professor was not listening to a word he was saying. The two of them,
the professor and the other man, it is true, sat down at Pareith's
table, but the Florentine simply kept on talking. At some point the
professor interrupted him. But in so doing, I have no reason to sys-
tematize anything, he said. He didn't care about the parameters. Even
if everything he was saying was possibly conclusive, he didn't give a
damn. That's my fundamental right too, don't you agree, Saverio,
that that is my fundamental right? Not to care about it? The professor was visibly upset, even though of course the other people listening understood nothing at all of what he was saying. Saverio: From
what is this fundamental right supposed to be derived? Is there a
fundamental right not to have to take note of things? Klein: But
those are all theories. Incidentally, all your dialectic is metaphysics.

All the conclusions of this sort of dialectic lead to purely imaginary products. What Nietzsche calls analysis I call mere fancy and a multiplicity of combinations. You take one thing, then another, combine the two, and then say whatever comes into your mind about the combination. That's what has always annoyed me about Nietzsche. Everything, free combination, but with a claim, with a claim, I ask you! Pareith was listening with great interest to Saverio and Klein's conversation, which was apparently about metaphysical questions (Nietzsche!); metaphysical questions held a very special fascination for the painter. I also occupy myself with these sorts of questions, he said, and looked ostentatiously at his cheroot. Saverio and Klein looked at him. But certainly, said Pareith. Being, movement, or the question: Is it all the same and unified, or is it not all the same and unified? These were questions that he also introduced into his art, or at least that he tried to introduce into his art; he aspired in his art, he said, to believe that such questions deserved to be introduced. Or, he said, he was interested, for example, in the question: Whether, in the final analysis, everything was contradictory, or not contradictory. Klein looked at Pareith aghast, then he went on talking. Pareith listened, completely spellbound, to the ensuing conversation about *metaphysics* and *Nietzsche* and *dialectic, et cetera*, although he did not understand a word of it, he did not even know, for example, what the two of them were talking about, and, above all, he did not know what it all had to do with Nietzsche. Saverio to Klein: That was exactly what he had wanted to say all the time, but he (Klein) did not want to understand him. Nietzsche did not describe things. Nietzsche deduced them. In this point he makes a distinction in culture, between the new conscious culture which *administers* the earth *economically as a whole*, and the old culture, where human beings were determined by their need, where need set limits for them as conditions required, just as it set limits for animals and plants, and so he calls this old culture a mere animal and plant life. Klein: But for him (Klein) the animal and plant life was considerably preferable. The earth cannot be administered economically; no system can tolerate such complexity, and above all no one person. It leads to murder and violence. Saverio: But that's exactly what he (Saverio) had been saying all the time. Nietzsche does not say, thus and thus is good, and thus and thus is bad, and you must do this and that, but he sees a new historical stage. This will simply come of itself; it will not depend, in any shape or form, upon the will of the individual, and the question as to whether the new stage will be better or worse or good or bad or functional or, as the case may be, non-functional simply does not arise. A meteor could just as well strike the earth. Nietzsche simply describes how the meteor strikes the earth, nothing else. Klein made a dismissive gesture with his two hands. He wagers, he said, on the individual, which means that he is historically out of date, but yet he wagers on the individual. The individual alone can be the measure of all things, not an economy. Saverio: The human being is his economy. His measure of all things is the economy. But no one has ever properly understood that. You cannot distinguish between the human being and economy, such a distinction is always artificial, *et cetera*. Now other people joined the two tables. A German named Badowsky had been in the Cellar for about a quarter of an hour; he had at first sat down for a short while next to Auer, but had then stood up again and gone outside, only to return after a few moments with a cigarette in his mouth, and now he was standing near the professor and eyeing him, his suit, and, above all, his tie respectfully. The German, named Badowsky, had been in Klausen for a few days; he seemed to be everywhere recently, but no one really knew what he was actually doing in Klausen. He had struck up an acquaintance with Auer; that is to say, they would drink together day in, day out, in the local bars, cadging drinks off people. Badowsky was unshaven, had long greasy hair, and wore a checked shirt that was carelessly buttoned. He had been wearing this shirt since he had arrived in Klausen; obviously he had no other. And he was very brown; apparently he spent a lot of time in the open air, lying in meadows or some such place, with crates of beer and bottles of schnapps. For some time now, Auer had been making friends with people of this sort; he had got to know many such people in Ploder castle in Brixen, perhaps Badowsky as well . . . Klein, in the meantime, was talking with Saverio Zanetti, who, as it transpired, was an assistant of Klein's in Bolzano, in charge of certain administrative details relating to the latter's full professorship. Badowsky stared obtrusively at the pair of them, curling up his lips derisively in the process; apparently he found the conversation the two were having completely idiotic. He looked as though he could not begin to understand that two people could talk about *administrative questions*. After a while he even sat down, immediately and ostentatiously, next to the professor. And so you are a professor? he suddenly asked between two of Klein's sentences. Klein looked at the suntanned man, but he did not answer, and he immediately turned back to Zanetti. This made the German fighting mad. Here, just a moment, he said, didn't I just ask you if you were a professor? What are you a professor of, then? Klein sat up straight. I'm a professor of X. Oh! said Badowsky, professor of X! And what does one do then as a professor of X? asked Badowsky. Look, said Professor Klein, we have a meeting tomorrow; we need to have discussed a few things beforehand, and that is what we are doing at the moment, so please let us get on with it. After saying this, he turned away again and brushed him off. So, a meeting, said Badowsky, unabashed, and stubbed his cigarette out, actually in the ashtray that was directly in front of Klein. And what sort of a meeting might that be? Klein: You would scarcely understand. Or do you understand what goes on in a university? Me? asked Badowsky. Of course I know what goes on in a university. I know my way around everywhere, and of course I know my way around people like you. A meeting! But this is a pub, man! He was now looking over at Auer. Yes, Auer, I know my way around, Badowsky repeated. I know it all. To the professor: And shall I tell you something, Herr Professor of X. It makes me sick. The professor looked the German in the face without saying a word and then turned away again. Badowsky left him alone then. Since he obviously had no money, he cadged a cigarette from someone, and after a little while he conferred with Auer as to whether the latter could arrange with the landlord for him to have credit. Auer then went outside. Gasser finally remembered the letter he had been carrying around with him all the time to give to Auer. It was a letter from Germany, from a ministry. However, Auer stayed outside for a time. Meanwhile Badowsky was suddenly sitting next to Professor Klein again. The man who was just here, he said to Professor Klein, that was Auer. Leopold Auer, you know! The professor said that may well be, he may be a Herr Leopold Auer, but he had not met him, and in any case there was nothing more to be said about it, would he please excuse him! Badowsky murmured something, and meanwhile he was fumbling about in his pants pocket, out of which he pulled a crumpled up piece of paper. With grave gestures and extremely formally, Badowsky smoothed out the paper and laid it on the table in front of the professor. He writes, said Badowsky. Aha, said Klein. Badowsky: He is a poet. Klein could do nothing but look mutely at the disheveled German again. He was just about to leave; he looked completely helpless. And since, said Badowsky, you are a professor, I would like to ask you what a professor would have to say, for example, about this. I say nothing about it, said Klein. I am a professor of X, not a literary scholar. Listen to that! cried Badowsky into the room, he is professor of X, but not a literary scholar. So, are the works of the poets written for literary scholars, so that they alone should read them? The professor was now completely floored by his conversation with Badowsky, and he was, at that moment in time, unable to find the right counter-argument. No, he said, of course not, all he wanted to say . . . er . . . Badowsky held out the paper to him again. Klein admitted defeat, took out his glasses, and relieved him of the smoothed-out piece of paper. Well, you know, he said, as he examined the piece of paper, a lot of people write. For example, people in the large German railway stations; I often frequent them—I mean, of course, out of necessity . . . can you imagine how many of them are writing, especially at night? They sit there with various pieces of paper, or exercise books, smoking, not wearing any socks, writing something with grave expressions on their faces; you see it every night. All these people consider themselves poets, even scholars, or mathematicians, and then they suddenly jump up and make speeches to the people; they are standing around somewhere, at a vending machine or on a bench, and suddenly they make their speeches. He was reading now. Then he handed the piece of paper back. And? asked Badowsky . . . Professor Klein said that unfortunately he could not make anything out; the writing was not clear. That's true, said Badowsky. He too had been unable to read anything. Auer really was very drunk when he wrote that. But he believed in Auer. So, said Klein, in order at last to get rid of the German, whom he found really repulsive. I have more of these slips of paper, said Badowsky, just a moment! Oh! Spare me for heaven's sake! cried Klein. Klein was now very upset, really angry, he was almost on his feet. He'd been talking at him for twenty minutes, he said, and he was completely drunk; he should go out into the street and make his speeches there, but should leave him, Klein, in peace. He hoped that he had finally expressed himself clearly. Badowsky laughed and looked Klein in the face, kindly and animatedly. He's also had poems published in the *Frankfurter Allgemeine Zeitung*, did you know that? Klein, feeling very weak: No, he didn't know. Badowsky: And he draws. He draws all the faces here, all the Klauseners, didn't you know that, for example? Klein: No, not that either. Badowsky: He could make a book out of them, but I don't think that he wants to. Whispering: He's a great man, but nobody knows it. Klein: Aha. Badowsky: I'm surprised that he treats it all as though it is so worthless, as though it were nothing, nothing at all; I even think he would rather throw everything away, he'd rather not have anything to do with them. He would actually rather have nothing at all to do with things like that; he is apparently completely beyond all that. In fact, Auer is beyond all that. He has already arrived somewhere else. That's why his poems cannot be understood, because he has arrived somewhere completely different. In incomprehensibility. It is only the incomprehensible that is comprehensible in incomprehensibility; he, Badowsky, had always known that. Klein: So, you knew that. Badowsky: Yes, obviously, that's why I never became a professor. Yes, said Klein, you're right about that. Badowsky now continued talking about Auer; his poems and his drawings; the comprehensible and the incomprehensible; the failure and all those who have not failed and who, in any event, represent what is most wretched on earth (for example, professors); and he became more and more entangled in a perpetual and completely insubstantial apologia of Auer and certain incomprehensible things. He said he had asked himself, at first, what Auer's poems were supposed to mean. Then he understood them. They meant nothing at all. But they are, nevertheless, poems, rejoined Klein, so they must also mean something. Badowsky slapped his thigh, laughed, and made a face like a happy horse. That's the whole art, cried Badowsky, the art is to write a poem that means nothing at all. He looked at Klein expectantly. Auer came back into the room. No, no, everything means something, said Professor Klein conscientiously. Badowsky: That's what you say. Listen to this, Auer, listen to what the professor of X is saying. Everything means something. Ha-ha, meanwhile I don't even know what that is supposed to mean, everything means something. Explain it to me! Klein: Of course everything means something. And if something rejects such a meaning, then . . . then . . . The professor was now aware that there was no greater mistake than arguing with this drunken vagabond. But the latter became more and more enthusiastic about his own statements. To mean nothing was the greatest possible purpose! Thus far he had understood Auer: namely, that there was no greater artistic achievement than meaning nothing. Nothingness, the actual purpose. To hell with everything, ha-ha! cried Badowsky, clapping his hands happily. Everyone looked at him aghast; a few were unnerved, for in the meantime Badowsky had become rather loud (he was also half standing on his table). Auer said nothing. It's all nonsense anyway, cried Badowsky, and therefore there is nothing, and because there is nothing my dear professor of the subject X, my friend Auer writes poems that mean nothing. That's the way it is, Auer, that's the way it is . . . incidentally I haven't any more beer. Isn't there anyone in this whole goddamn bar who can give me a beer? Shit (he turned out his pants pockets). Then it grew quiet for a while. Conversations were once more confined to individual tables. Now, at last, Gasser took the letter from the German ministry out of his pocket. The letter, which was addressed to Auer, had been sent to Gasser's address because, for a time now, Auer had not had a permanent address; sometimes he slept at Ploder castle, sometimes at Sonja's or Gasser's, but now that it was summertime he slept outside more and more often, no one could say exactly where, probably below the monastery. He would also frequently spend the night in a small toolshed on the other side of the valley. In any case, he had most recently also had a tiny room right above the Cellar. Gasser sat down next to Auer at the table and lay the aforementioned letter down on it. Leopold Auer looked at the letter in surprise and picked it up after a while, so that he could turn it over and see more clearly who the sender was. Then he opened it. He read the letter through several times, his face becoming more and more contorted, then he laid the letter down again and several people asked: What was in the letter? Auer looked thoughtfully at Gasser. Then he stood up and sat down on one of the empty barrels. No one understood why he was behaving like this, above all Badowsky. The German took the letter and read it through, from top to bottom, but did not seem to understand it properly. And, Moreth asked, what's in it? No idea, said Badowsky. He had not, he said, been able to concentrate on reading all this stuff, he couldn't even follow the first sentence. Those sentences, these people express everything so strangely, it's absolutely unreal. What sort of people work in these civil service offices! said Badowsky. He wanted nothing to do with it; Badowsky threw the letter onto the table. He felt insecure now about the whole situation; he had nothing left to drink. Auer was sitting on his own on the barrel, not wanting to talk to anyone any more, so he took a deep breath, cast a derogatory glance at all those present, and left. What the letter contained was not immediately revealed. The Klauseners only found out much later. Incidentally, it was subsequently said that Auer, on his barrel, had begun some sort of sketch on a paper napkin that evening, possibly one of the *pazzi* for which people would later have gladly drawn and quartered him. Whenever Klauseners talked about Auer later on, they recalled situations in which Auer is supposed to have drawn such *pazzi*, but only after his room above the Cellar had been broken into. It was even asserted that, sitting on the barrel that evening, Auer had drawn the *mayor*, in fact, very accurately, either from memory and by using his vivid imagination, or because he had been present that same afternoon when the mayor had given a speech to some guild or other, but these were all unproven allegations. But later, in spite of (or perhaps because of) his illness, Auer was accused of all sorts of things; he was made into a catalyst of the event, and, as late as when his room was broken into, people had still regarded him as one of the chief culprits, someone who, more than anyone else, had poisoned and disturbed the peace of the community and had provided fertile intellectual and aesthetic ground on which the terror could flourish. But Auer was a completely innocent person, who until the end did not properly understand what had actually happened to him when he had run on to the autobahn bridge just behind the Klausen exit. Auer never wished, nor intended, to cause any harm with his napkins; he regarded himself as a completely independent artist. To this day, there is a napkin hanging in Castle Sigmundskron that depicts the mayor as a *pazzo*; everyone can see it because Auer is a poster child for the Eisack valley. But this napkin bears a quite different date. Auer had drawn it twelve months before the evening when he was supposed to have drawn it. This meant, therefore, that everything stemmed from spiteful gossip, even if most people considered it the established truth. At that time people would not have taken Auer seriously but would have considered him an ordinary village idiot, if he had not already published several poems in respected German periodicals and newspapers (his best-known poem was a long poem of about thirty lines; it was called ***, and is today a sort of national anthem of the Klauseners; even the mayor can quote from it of late). Thanks to this, Auer had achieved a certain fame in his own lifetime. He was not understood, but people were consoled by the fact that other people understood him (the newspaper editors), and they, the Klauseners told themselves, were in a much better position to judge than they, the Klauseners themselves, were. At the time, Auer mostly wrote his poems for a glass of wine. Everybody thought this odd (today they put on airs if they had once happened to sit two tables away from him in the same restaurant, and tell their stories). At that time most of them didn't even bother to save Auer's poems, something they now regard as a philological catastrophe; for nowadays

Auer is considered, even by the Provincial governor, to be the most important and most famous poet that the Eisack valley has ever produced—admittedly, he is also, of course, long since dead (officially of a liver embolism as a result of neglected hepatitis). And even if Auer, once the alleged rebel, is now venerated by the Klauseners by acts of commemoration, exhibitions, and seminars, *et cetera*, he is, on the other hand, thanks to the events of the time, still a much disputed figure, and at the moment the Klauseners are arguing as to whether the school on the Eisack should be renamed the Leopold Auer High School, some are strongly in favor, others at least as strongly opposed. Gasser and Sonja left the Cellar after a while. This evening in the Cellar was later considered important and seminal, and it was described over and over again, until it had become completely falsified. The same was true of the conversation on economics, dialectic, and Nietzsche (a further intellectual incendiarist) between the professor and his assistant, and a significance and singularity were ascribed to Badowsky's remarks about nothingness and incomprehensibility, which, like almost everything in Klausen, was a retrospective interpretation, a perception *post festum*—a decisive form of cognition for the Klauseners which is, however, completely meaningless, since in Klausen it bears fruit only as nonsense, just as it does everywhere else in the world. Gasser and Sonja walked from the Cellar to the Eisack and sat down together on a bench on the square in front of their old school, opposite the hill on the other side of the river and a hundred meters from the bridge. Everything was bathed in a yellow light, because in Klausen everything was permanently floodlit for the sake of the tourists, so that the famous and picturesque buildings could be seen from the autobahn, in the hope that next time people would

decide to make a detour into Klausen and leave their money there.
And, while Sonja and Gasser were sitting on the bench, they witnessed an event which, on the following morning and in the days
afterwards, was also described in Klausen in a number of very different ways, an event which afterwards turned out to be the beginning
of a whole series of violent clashes and which, as a result, was to
involve the police. There were two arrests, though on the following
morning several people's, including Sonja's, personal details were
checked and a few summonses were issued. Gasser's name was not
mentioned at first, for in fact he and Sonja were just as surprised by
the whole business as most other people. This clash on the square in
front of the school only makes sense if we look back a few days. A
short time before, a town meeting had taken place in the community
center at which a group belonging to party X had introduced a proposal that had long been a subject of public discussion in Klausen.
This stated that as a result of the continual increase of traffic on the
Brenner autobahn (especially *in the sphere of heavy freight traffic*, as it
was called in the proposal) and of the constant increase in noise allied
to this; it was proposed that a series of measurements be made at
different public points in Klausen, at various times of the day and
night, and also in private residences which were particularly affected,
et cetera. Behind these formulations of the proposal, which were as
usual tortuously expressed, stood, to make a long story short, the
wish of a few Klauseners to have the noise in the town measured so
as to ascertain whether the noise, as measured, still conformed with
the noise reduction statutes and the operating permit of the autobahn.
The question as to what should happen if the noise (many people
spoke not of noise but only of sound) exceeded the permitted level

had already been voiced in a meeting of the town council. Should one write to the Italian authorities with the request that the autobahn be shut? This request by Alderman Moreth caused a certain amusement among the group of opponents of the proposal. Some considered the proposal superfluous, others annoying. For example, people were disputing whether the proposal should talk of noise emission at all, or only of sound emission, for some people were still not sure if what the *sphere of heavy freight traffic* (many said *the heavy traffic sector*) emitted up there on the autobahn was noise or sound. Some said that the word noise was already an interpretation of the sounds, although the determination as to whether these sounds were in fact noise could only be made after the measurements had been taken. Others became agitated at the sophistries that were uttered, admittedly in a some-what amused tone, and said that, of course, what was heard from the autobahn was noise, what else was it if you were unable to sleep at night on the Eisack side even if your windows were closed? A wild storm of shouting immediately broke out. Then the person concerned should sleep on the other side of the house, said Alderman Mitter-rutzner. Or: The person concerned was a nervous person, that had nothing to do with the sphere of heavy freight traffic, that was more to do with his own nervous dysfunction. The person concerned had already attracted attention as a troublemaker. He always found some-thing to complain about, no matter what . . . The mayor tried to find some way of smoothing things out between these heated voices, and in fact there were a number of people who said the matter should be treated in a civilized manner. However, other voices were louder, those of the aggressive supporters and those of the uncompromising opponents. What was the person concerned to do, asked Alderman X, if only one room, and that one on the Eisack side, were available and thus there was absolutely no other possibility open to him but to sleep on that side? Interjection by alderman Y: He, Y, had always slept well even on the Eisack side; voice of dissent to X: The person concerned should sit down on the seat of his pants, earn some money, and buy himself a place to live somewhere else if he didn't want live on the Eisack . . . The arguments of the supporters of the proposition were, at first, more or less as follows: The noise must be contained, the Klauseners' quality of life must be improved. The opposition: Klausen had a very high quality of life, there was no noise. The proposers now began to support their argument with medical opinions, which contained expressions like nervous damage, *et cetera*, and added the suggestion that the tourist trade also called for a reduction of noise in the town. The more quiet it was, the more tourists would come to the town, and that would be good for the economy. The other side dismissed this argument out of hand and said that most places in Klausen were totally quiet, no one experienced nervous damage, no one heard anything, and it would give a totally false signal to the economy if truck traffic were to be reduced. The climate in the Eisack valley was already regarded as sufficiently hostile to the economy, they were already notorious in the whole of Europe. At this, a part of the faction of the party making the proposal lost its composure. In a speech that lasted at least twenty minutes, Alderman Valli enumerated all the highway construction projects in the Eisack valley during the previous ten years—obviously he had learned them all by heart beforehand and had only awaited this opportunity; no one present at the meeting had ever heard of most of the projects he mentioned. What, a road between X and Y? Where might this X and this Y be? And why had a road been built there, and above all what on earth did this have to do with Klausen? *Et cetera*. People shouted out this, and other things like it. For a short time the meeting seemed to descend into chaos. It was then time for a vote, and the proposal was defeated by fifteen votes to nine. The next day, the citizens' action group, *Noise Protection of Klausen*, was formed in the mayor's office. Within a few days the group attracted a mass membership, drawn from all those who lived down by the Eisack. Even the woman who owned Branzoll, it was said, was interested in the project. That was also not a surprise; after all Branzoll is the same height as the bridge over the valley, which had been built on the hill opposite, and people were surprised that the nuns from the convent had shown no interest in the matter, for it was precisely up there, a hundred and fifty meters higher than Branzoll, where people must have absolutely hated the bridge. Even Professor Klein joined the action group, and people learned something of his tale of woe. Klein was teaching for a semester in Bolzano, and just a few days after he started he had given up the apartment that the university had put at his disposal and had moved to Klausen, because Bolzano was too noisy for him and he had had an idyllic image of Klausen in his mind. This idyllic image obviously only derived from the fact that prior to his arrival he had known nothing more of the Eisack valley than the well-known engraving by Albrecht Dürer, *The Great Happiness*, that shows Klausen in the background and which has helped the town to make a international name for itself in art history circles. Admittedly, Dürer saw the town a few centuries before our day, and what Klein found on his arrival was an enormous autobahn bridge, constant village festivals with loud pop-music, and a neighbor who watched TV morning and night, and who Klein—whose nerves were nearly shattered—took to court after only a week. Klein was, by the way, not someone given to complaining, but he had that effect upon people. Several voices within the action group were soon raised, proclaiming certain things that Alderman Taschner could not brook. For many people the autobahn at once became a symbol of the Italian state. The following comparison was made: just as the Italian state had destroyed Bolzano by militantly industrializing it, thus destroying the whole Bolzano basin and making in uninhabitable for decades to come (the whole place, they said, was full of Italians), so it had built the A22 for exactly the same purpose. With the A22 the Italian state had finally annexed the Eisack valley and debased it, turning it into a transit region. That, they said, was something that people simply had not understood when the autobahn was built and everyone was happy about it . . . Others disagreed and pointed out that the autobahn did not belong to the state, but was owned by a private company, admittedly with the participation of the South Tyrolean government, and the economic prosperity of South Tyrol was due to the advent of the autobahn. Against this it was said that the economic prosperity of South Tyrol was only a leash that the Italians had put round the necks of the South Tyroleans. If the South Tyroleans had not placed so great a value on prosperity, there would long ago have been murder and manslaughter there, and they would have long since thrown the Italians out of their country. It seemed as though after only two days a serious quarrel broke out within the ranks of the newly established citizens' action group. Among the old people, who had lived through the Option Period in South Tyrol,[1] there were those who chose Italy and those who chose South Tyrol, and a few who chose South Tyrol also immediately left the action group; however, at the last moment Taschner succeeded, at least temporarily, in smoothing things out. The action group *Noise Protection of Klausen* decided to undertake noise measurements on its own, that is, without a ruling by the town council. The village of Blumau was contacted and inquiries were made about the scientific criteria for, and the technical procedures involved in, making such measurements. Gruber, the owner of the electrical goods shop in the lower town, an acquaintance of Josef Gasser, who was also often to be seen in the Cellar, was sent to Blumau to inspect the instruments. Gruber discovered that the instruments were on loan from a German technical emergency service, so he went to Nuremberg, where the instruments came from, and started negotiations. In Nuremberg, they insisted that the instruments could only be loaned if a ruling had been made by the town council, as it had been in Blumau. Gruber returned to Klausen with this newly acquired knowledge. Thereupon Taschner made a few telephone calls. He discovered that the Italian Ministry of the Environment made these instruments available on the basis of a ruling of the town council. He then inquired in Blumau as to why they had not requested the instruments from the Italian ministry but from the Nuremberg address. It seemed suspicious to him. Finally, it

---

1. The period between 1939 and 1943 when the non-Italian speaking people living in South Tyrol were given the "option" of either emigrating to Hitler's Germany or remaining in South Tyrol and being forcefully integrated into the mainstream Italian culture, losing their language and cultural heritage.

transpired that no such council ruling had been made in Blumau, thus making it impossible to approach the ministry, and they had presented the emergency technical service in Nuremberg with incomplete documentation. This created a scandal in Blumau, for after the results of the measurements that had been made in Blumau were published—they were catastrophic—the town council subsequently simply said that they themselves had ordered the measurements to be taken, although the opposite had been the case: they had tried to stop them (as being harmful to the economy). A few days later the instruments from Nuremberg were available. Gasser was approached and asked whether he would not undertake to direct the noise measurement project—because it was believed that he had gained experience when running such 'campaigns' in Berlin—but Gasser merely burst out laughing when he was asked and indicated to councilor Taschner that he thought him crazy. On the day he was asked, Gasser—purely out of demoscopic interest—took soundings among members of the action group. Many of them seemed to him to be in a very good mood, and in the majority of cases he was unable to find out why they had become members of the group. For some of them, for example, it seemed merely a question of which party they belonged to. Among other things, Gasser discovered that almost all the protesters owned cars. At least thirty of the some fifty members of the citizens action group *Noise Protection of Klausen* even commuted daily by car. They traveled to Bolzano every day, and Gasser was often witness to a telling argument: whoever traveled from Klausen to Bolzano entered the autobahn after Klausen; thus they did not drive past Klausen, and therefore did not contribute in any way to noise pollution in Klausen. However, it was extremely embarrassing to be confronted with the fact that everyone who traveled to Bolzano also passed by Blumau. Meanwhile, Blumau had served them all, in the preceding discussion, as an example of abuse due to noise and exhaust-gas pollution . . . The measurements by the citizen's action group began three days after the unsuccessful proposal in the town council. Gruber and Sonja Maretsch's brother, Christian, undertook them. They rang the bells of all the residents down by the Eisack, some of them let them into their houses, whereas others did not. Some of the families who were complaining about the autobahn did not want to have Maretsch and Gruber in their houses in the middle of the night; others, however, thought that it was important, because the noise of the trucks was greater at night, as a disproportionately large number of them traveled at night compared with the daytime. Maretsch and Gruber worked most enthusiastically, and in the first night alone took measurements in almost a dozen dwellings. For instance they rang Family X's—with whom they had previously spoken—bell at three o'clock in the morning, installed the measuring instruments in the bedroom, after which they spent a time measuring, first with the window open and then with it closed. Gruber and Maretsch then quickly packed everything up and rang the bell at the next house, where they were already expected; it was now half past three in the morning, and so the pair of them plodded away almost around the clock. Of course there were arguments. One night on the stairs, for instance, old Herr Perluttner shouted in a loud voice that the two of them were scoundrels and communists, for as far as Perluttner was concerned anyone who was anti-German and who spoke out for Italy was a communist—for some reason or another, he considered the measurements to be something South Tyrolean that was anti-German

and pro-Italian. Perluttner wakened the whole house with his hue
and cry. Perluttner had been waiting all night for the two of them to
appear to make their measurements, wrapped in a woolen blanket
and provided with a thermos of coffee; he had been waiting for them
behind the door of his little apartment, deep in a journal called *German Dispatch Riders from 1914 to 1945.* When he heard them on the
stairs ringing the so and so family's bell, he stormed out—it was
already almost half past four in the morning—and cussed them out
like a drill sergeant. He also boxed Gruber's ears with his journal; the
latter took it all in stride because he said to himself that the last thing
the citizens' action group *Noise Protection of Klausen* could use at the
moment was an excess of force. The next day, Perluttner even wanted
to press charges—about something or other—against the two, and
he wrote a bitter and angry letter to the *Eisacktaler Tagblatt*, but the
local police did not press the charges; in fact, Perluttner was sent
back home . . . On the night in question, while Gasser and Sonja were
sitting in the square in front of the school, Gruber and Sonja's brother
wanted to take measurements in some of the public places. Both of
them were completely tired out after the exertions of the previous few
days, because they still had their normal work to do during the day,
Gruber in his electrical supply shop and Christian Maretsch as a
vocational-school teacher. They came to the square with their cables
and their boxes at about midnight and began to erect their instruments. A few pubs were closing at this hour, several cars were driving through Klausen's narrow streets, passers-by appeared, there was
a certain amount of unrest. Gruber and Maretsch were caught up in
a discussion with some drunks. Gruber asked the people to walk on,
for if they were to stay around here talking to one another, the two of

them would not be able measure the noise made by the trucks up above on the autobahn. Why not? people asked. Answer: Because each word deflected the decibel meter. Counter answer: In that case every word was louder than the trucks up above. Gruber now attempted to explain to the people that, of course, that was not the case, or at least only relatively so. The others however insisted that they were the ones disturbing the peace and not the trucks, so Gruber should be measuring them, not the trucks. Gruber: You must move on now, he had work to do. The group: they wanted to be measured at once. They wanted to be measured on the spot. It took Gruber and Maretsch a while to get rid of these people again. Around one o'clock in the morning it had grown relatively quiet, and they were now able to make notes of results. But then another group of people appeared. These people were in an excitable mood from the outset and were evidently intent on an open confrontation. Then, strikingly, Laner suddenly appeared, and with him, in his entourage, Martin Delazer. Laner tried to cool things down, but Maretsch, who had, in the course of the affair, been badly knocked about (as had alderman Moreth), said later that Laner's attempt to cool things down had merely been a diversionary maneuver; Laner had merely wanted to divert attention from the fact that, presumably, he himself was behind the brutal group who had appeared on the scene. The details of what happened were as follows. First of all, an unknown South Tyrolean came up to Maretsch and involved him in a conversation about a random topic. At some point in the conversation the man started to talk about the measuring apparatus—What is it? he asked, apparently eager to find out. Maretsch explained that the object in question was a decibel meter. The man continued to inquire interestedly, but with an increasingly aggressive undertone in his voice, and while this was going on, a few more people, South Tyroleans unknown to Maretsch, appeared on the scene. They wanted to know whether he could produce something to prove that he was authorized to take measurements here, where he had gotten the measuring apparatus from, whether he had a permit, *et cetera*. Maretsch and Gruber said they could do as they pleased here, it was a free country and this was a public place. At this, the mysterious group began to laugh and to smirk, they found the term *free country* particularly funny; here and there fists were clenched. Meanwhile it had become obvious to Maretsch and Gruber that the group intended to beat them up and destroy the instruments, and that the reason everyone who had appeared there, as if by chance, in the square in front of the school at one o'clock in the morning, was unknown to them, was merely because they had been hired from out of town. Maretsch and Gruber therefore took up positions with their backs to the instruments. One of the strangers was just about to touch the meter when something happened that the unknown people had obviously not reckoned with. Another group, consisting of people drawn from the aforementioned faction of the opponents of the proposition, appeared on the square. Apparently, they had already made plans, in a pub, to meet with the two people who were doing the measuring and involve them in a discussion to dissuade them from making the measurements. What happened was inevitable. The new arrivals—with completely peaceful intentions—immediately stationed themselves between Maretsch and Gruber and the others and tried to persuade the group of out-of-towners to abandon their violent intentions, while they, for their part, involved the thugs in a discussion. The group of thugs was confused and disgruntled by this, and, for no other reason than that of bad temper and impatience, one of the strangers punched Moreth in the face. Moreth fell to the ground, bleeding, and a general brawl ensued. Gasser and Sonja, who had long been watching from their bench in front of the school, now also joined in. Gruber phoned his brother to come at once with the car and secure the instruments. Gasser was seeing to Moreth and was trying to hold a handkerchief to his nose, but Moreth was crying out in pain, because his nose had been broken by the punch. Someone from the mysterious group must also have telephoned, for Laner and Delazer suddenly appeared. Delazer's secretary and two or three others from Laner's closest circle were suddenly in the square. Everyone immediately calmed down and stayed still; people made room for Laner wherever he went. Delazer kept in the background. Incidentally, nobody gave a thought as to how Laner—who for days had been in hiding—suddenly appeared just like that at half past one in the morning. What's going on here? he asked, as though he represented law and order in the square. People were talking back and forth, and the members of the gang of hired thugs were all gazing up into the night sky and denying everything. Laner saw Moreth, who was huddled on the ground, and asked what had happened. A misunderstanding, it was said, a mere misunderstanding, someone had possibly misunderstood a word that Moreth had said and someone had gotten mad at him, but it was not certain who it was, *et cetera*. Laner reprimanded all those present and said to Gruber that this had all arisen because of the unnecessary measurements, they were as superfluous as a goiter, people should not be provoked unnecessarily and it was very irresponsible to be using these expensive instruments at night, especially in public places, *you never know how it may end up.* Then he left the square again, a bare three minutes after he had first put in an appearance. Delazer, who had not said a word the whole time but had been watching the crowd searchingly, as though wanting to take exact note of every face, again followed in his footsteps. The others followed. Maretsch, Gasser, and Gruber gazed after Laner, Kati's fiancé, and the others in astonishment. And now everything happened in a rush. Gruber's brother arrived with a delivery van; the instruments were stowed away; Gasser and Sonja helped the two Grubers; and at that moment, while everyone was more or less occupied doing something or other and the aldermen were engaged in a heated argument, the group of hired thugs knocked Christian Maretsch down—he had been standing off to one side—and someone suddenly had a cudgel in his hands and was using it to rain blows on the prostrate man's skull, while two or three others quickly joined in. Since it all took, at most, two or three seconds, no one could intervene. Then the hired thugs started shouting again: *That all happened just because the Klauseners are so unreasonable . . .* and then they were gone. Now, of course, everyone was in a state of utter confusion. Christian Maretsch was in great pain and his forehead was bleeding; Gruber and Gasser immediately drove him and Moreth, still groaning, to the emergency room in Brixen. And so the night ended with everyone in a state of shock. The next day, after the incident had become known, Gasser was spoken to in the street on several occasions; oddly enough, people shouted certain things after him, which he had to interpret as hostile although he had had nothing to do with the night's happenings, he simply chanced to have been witness to what had happened, nothing more. The hostility towards Gasser was very vague, along the lines of: He should not drive a wedge between the Klauseners . . . He had been away so long he did not understand what was happening, he no longer understood the Klauseners, everything had grown strange to him, *et cetera*. People said similar things about Sonja. Gasser was somewhat confused about it, because he was of course not aware of being guilty in any shape or form. He went into the Cellar and there he was confronted—it was about midday—by a body of Klauseners engaged in a hot debate; incidentally, more or less, the same people who had been in the Cellar on the previous evening. Now, however they were sitting in the front room. Carafes were standing around, people were cutting up bacon here and there, the white tablecloths were strewn with breadcrumbs, there was a certain tension in the air: it was like being at a political debate or even a briefing. Pareith appeared shocked at the night's events, inasmuch as they had been described to him; he was puffing on his cheroot and said that something should be done. But he was not in a position to say what (and for what or against what). Laner's role was discussed, not only in the events of the day before, but as a whole in Klausen. Some supported him and said Laner had created a lot of jobs for the South Tyroleans. Others said he was corrupt and a crook and that all the people who provide jobs, insofar as they are not jobs in the minor or mid-level crafts, are criminals and corrupt. None of these people cared about giving work to the South Tyroleans, all they wanted was to use the South Tyroleans for their own profit. What had Laner built in the Sarn valley? A paper mill, said others, and a lot of people had been employed there. But, some asked, was the paper needed? Where had it been sold? Had anyone suffered a shortage of paper anywhere? Answer: No. All right, so he had cut down almost the whole forest out there,

Point one, and, Point two, he had built a quite senseless factory, and what's more, Point three, with bank loans, and now, Point four, everything had been liquidated, the mill was rotting, all the jobs had gone, nobody had Laner to thank for a job now, but the valley had been destroyed and disfigured. The others: But for years they did have Laner to thank for work. There had suddenly been work, where previously there had been none. Better for a few years than never. And if people had not put every stumbling block that you could possibly imagine in Laner's and the Sarn valley dwellers' way, then the mill would still be there and there would still be work. Thus it went back and forth. Some argued with all their might on one side and others on the other, as they had done a thousand times in recent years. Taschner said they must get to the bottom of the previous night's violence, attention must also be paid as to whether the police were really working on clearing the matter up or whether they were putting it off, but of course one thing they did not want, one thing definitely, was an excessive use of force. No, some people shouted, they did not want that, and Klausen was certainly not the place for that. The Klauseners were peaceful people. They wanted peace. Exactly, someone shouted, they wanted work and peace. Critical voices were now raised against Taschner; he was accused of economic hostility because of his citizens' action group. Taschner defended himself to the best of his knowledge and belief. He spoke from the bottom of his heart and took up a position against the traffic, but all that could be repeated a thousand times and written down anew every time; all the conversations that people could have had about such subjects had taken place a thousand times and they never change. Of course, they are carried on every day. Some people are for something and others are against it, and the world goes on its way in spite of it all. Gasser interjected saying that . . . don't misunderstand me . . . he did not wish to speak for or against the citizens' action group. (Others: Why not? Why not for it? Why not against it? Why not, if he wanted to, speak against it? . . .) Gasser: All he wanted to say was as follows. The traffic would increase, like it or not, it had always increased and it would continue to increase just as a matter of course. He was immediately annoyed at himself for having said this, because it was a truism. Of course it was immediately seen as an opinion. Some reckoned that Gasser, in saying this, was against the citizens' action group, others reckoned that he was for it and that he should be made part of the group, for he would act far more radically than Taschner, who, according to many people, had done nothing at all but had, after a few days, handed the operative side of the business over to Gruber and only lent his name as the founder of the group. What was also striking was the appearance of Professor Klein and his wife. Klein's wife had arrived in Klausen the previous evening, intending to stay for the weekend. She was one of those Germans who love the South Tyrol better than anything and whose greatest pleasure is sitting in the open air on a hotel terrace at a wooden table, eating meat fritters or some other South Tyrolean dish, and looking at the mountains and the sky. She, above all, was delighted that Klein had accepted the one-year professorship in Bolzano. Both of them had been in the small wine-growing village of Girlan about ten years previously, had stayed for three days in a guesthouse, and eaten every day on the terrace of the *Marklhof*—to this day that was for Frau Klein the ultimate pleasure. True, in the *Marklhof*—and that's the point—you do not find typical South Tyrolean dishes, the cuisine is international.

Frau Dr. Klein, for example, loved steak tartare, which was mixed at the table with all sorts of herbs and spices by a slim, young, and very attractive waiter with skillful movements of his hands. Anyway, Frau Dr. Klein had arrived in Klausen late the previous evening, had installed herself on the balcony of her husband's apartment, breathed in what she considered the wonderful air, and sat looking at the mountains, that is she looked in the direction where the mountains were presumably to be found, because it was, after all, night time. And then they started arguing, or were at least annoyed, about certain things, and this ill humor lasted until the next day. Klein was sitting sullenly at a table in the front room of the Cellar, listening to the arguments between Taschner and the others, absent-mindedly crumbling a roll over the breadbasket. His wife was talking enthusiastically to the South Tyroleans and was very interested in everything connected with the night before. She was especially interested in Laner, for everyone represented him as the key figure in almost everything that happened in Klausen. She was talking about—and this upset the professor all the more—certain things that had to do with her work. Frau Dr. Klein worked in an institute for media research and had recently developed a project entitled *The Culture of Resistance on the World Wide Web*. She probably only started talking about the project because the citizens' action group, *Noise Protection of Klausen*, was also a form of resistance. In any case, she was talking about other people who were resisting other things, for example (and this, above all, was what upset the professor) the Frankfurt airport and the protest movement directed against it on the internet. Frau Dr. Klein was relating the strangest things, and a lot of people in the Cellar could not believe what radical forms of resistance there were (at least on the pages of the internet). The most common pages were those that just gave information about this and that. For example, the flight paths in the affected area had recently been rerouted and there was information about that; and, as is always the case, some people said one thing about the new flight paths, others another. But then there were also games that could be downloaded. Airliners could be shot down by means of an anti-aircraft gun controlled from a residential block; you earned considerably more points for shooting down Lufthansa planes than for those of other airlines, and if the plane broke up and you were told by the game that the plane had been on its way to Majorca, you received bonus points, and a heroic melody into the bargain. Then there were so-called discussion forums, in which every conceivable sort of passenger was insulted; every passenger, it was hoped, would be visited by the same hell which some people had to endure every day, because the others were constantly flying over their heads. There were handbooks on militant resistance and Frau Dr. Klein was also talking about a screenplay that someone had put on the net—the home security service had since removed it. It was the script for a film in which a suicide squad, similar to the one in *The Wild Geese* perhaps, captures the Frankfurt airport in a lightning attack and causes all sorts of destruction there, until, at the end, fighter planes appear from somewhere and completely destroy the airport. Frau Dr. Klein told this all with great amusement, for it apparently had great anecdotal value for her; she liked telling of people's strange and absurd eccentricities, it made her feel happy and contented. A lot of people really did laugh at what she told them in the Cellar; especially Badowsky, who had come in when she was in the middle of her stories and had listened enthralled and thoughtfully, just as though he were personally profiting from the stories. But the professor suddenly stood up and left because he could stand it no longer. Frau Dr. Klein looked up at the ceiling and sighed. At first she was about to follow him, then thought better of it. She couldn't always be running after him, she said, she too was only human, not just him. Was it her fault that their dispositions differed? People did not properly understand what the woman was saying. What was the matter with her husband? someone asked her. In a few words she now told her husband's life story, and hers too, which contained, among other things: the fact that her husband came from the Odenwald, that they lived near Frankfurt, that they had moved four times because of his sensitivity to noise, that he could not stand cars and, more recently, airplanes, that they had therefore decided to go to Bolzano for a year, but that there were also cars here now and that his neighbor started watching television at seven in the morning, *et cetera*. Indeed, doesn't the professor want to hear anything at all? people asked. She: That's just what she asks herself sometimes. He says over and over again that people should be quiet for once. Often, she said, when the fit is particularly bad, he just sits there, not reacting at all, muttering to himself, *Everyone . . . should finally be quiet*, over and over, *Everyone should finally be quiet*. That, she said, was frightening. The others: Yes, that was frightening. She: Last evening she had simply stood out on the balcony, just to enjoy the South Tyrolean air, but her husband had ordered her to close the balcony door, because of the cars. What cars? she had asked. You have to be quiet in order to hear them, he had said, then you will hear them. She had been quiet and then she really did hear the cars. If she closed the balcony door, the cars were noticeably quieter. All right, she said, just leave the balcony door closed. That's why I've come to Klausen is it, he said, in order to close the balcony door! She: There are cars everywhere. He: He knew that. She: You are pitting yourself against the whole human race. He: What nonsense. She: And that's why you're always quarreling with Saverio Zanetti recently. He's noticed that about you. You take exception to what people want, to everything they do that's new. You only tolerate what was already there before your time. Trains for example. You even used to tolerate the brickworks in *** stätten. Do you actually know what a noise that brickworks used to make, as early as about six-thirty in the morning, and that didn't bother you, you always slept with your windows open and used to say that the Odenwald, the Odenwald, you said, was magnificent. And you used to listen to the birds, and the little brook at your parent's house . . . He: The rustling of the leaves in the apple trees . . . She: Yes the rustling of the leaves in the apple trees, but you didn't hear the brickworks, you didn't take any notice of them, as far as you were concerned they were a natural sound, but I couldn't sleep in your parents' house for the noise of that damn brickworks. And when the workers arrived early in the morning on their bicycles, still half drunk, and started shouting filth and stupidity at one another, he didn't get upset (but she!). It was only when the workers started coming by car and after the parking lot had been built and the workers had all parked there in the morning and gone away again in the evening and when, at midday, a car had driven off here and there, it was only then that the Odenwald had been spoiled for him. Nowadays they no longer shout in the morning, they no longer exchange obscenities, because each comes in his own car; overall it had become more bearable (for her!), but as far as he was concerned this had wrecked the whole Odenwald and his parents' house. Then he had no longer wanted the house, *et cetera*, and now his brother was happily installed in it and he, Klein, went from place to place, each time entering into the next and deeper stage of despair. He: Right, so now the balcony doors are closed. Now will you be quiet? She: Why should she always be quiet? He: There, can't you hear that? She: What? He: That, do listen for heaven's sake. She: Yes. As a matter of fact. A television. She could hear a television. He: If I open the balcony door, I don't hear a television, I hear cars. If I close the balcony door again, I no longer hear the cars, but I do hear the television. A beautiful chiasmus. The chiasmus of my misfortune. Of my whole blighted existence. Badowsky: Had he tried Ohropax? Last month, he, Badowsky, had been living next door to a building site where they were excavating a foundation pit and Ohropax had helped. Frau Klein: What was he doing next to a foundation pit? Badowsky: What was he doing there? Nothing. They had been there for a time. There was a tent, someone or other had had a tent. There was always beer there too. It was a good time, he could recommend it to anyone. But here all people thought about were their health insurance and their pension, they didn't live. Perluttner to Frau Klein: What do you actually mean by good South Tyrolean air? You seat yourself on a balcony in Klausen and think you are breathing good South Tyrolean air? But the air isn't good. It is downright bad. That's because of the Italian cars. Others: Why Italian cars? We're no longer at war. It comes from cars in general, from the autobahn. Perluttner: German cars are cleaner. The Germans are cleaner in general. The South Tyrolean is basically a clean human being. Only the Italians, they make everything dirty here. They Italianize everything here. Perluttner pronounced the word *Italianized* in a long, drawn-out, nasalized fashion, maliciously and disparagingly. People explained to Frau Klein about the air-quality measurements that had recently been taken in the Eisack valley and told her that it was unfortunately the case that in most areas of the country, in Italy, Austria, and Germany, the air was markedly better than here. The Eisack valley was no longer a place for asthmatics, *et cetera*. Pareith said that in his opinion all this was only the result of modern methods of measurement. Today, everything is measured very accurately, and previously they didn't measure at all, and so now people think that everything is worse, whereas it is probably just the same as it always was. Other people now also dared to open their mouths and dispute the bad air quality. The air was not bad at all. If one went up a little higher onto the alpine pastures, the air there was the best air of any. The conversation went back and forth, and at some point the talk turned to Laner and his circle. People tried to determine how much of a role Delazer had played in the previous day's happenings. It had been noticed that he had kept in the background the whole time. This might have led people to conclude that Delazer had played a more passive role. Others said that perhaps it might lead you to conclude that Delazer had played an especially active role. Delazer, they maintained, had changed. The man who had stood for all that was rough and ready had become the man who kept in the background, holding the reins in his hand. Delazer in the meantime was *de facto* doing Laner's business. Laner, it was said, was growing old; his time in prison and the public's hostility had left a heavy mark upon him and had wounded him more deeply than people had previously thought. Perluttner: The man had always been careful of his honor. He himself had nothing to reproach him with. He had done a lot for all of them.

Without him, for example, there would be no sports center. The Italians had not wanted to give us a sports center, they do not want us South Tyroleans to toughen ourselves up, but we do. We build our own sports centers. Young Moreth said he found Delazer's athleticism repellent. Besides, he was almost fifty. You only have to look at his neck, the neck gives everything away. Delazer was also so brown, even his haircut had a certain something about it. He was the South Tyrolean Haider. He was striving with all his might to achieve a stronger and stronger position in the South Tyrolean parliament. And for that reason he had to stay in the background in things that affected Laner. Besides, people were far from knowing what exactly had happened the previous night. The police had not yet been able to apprehend anyone. Certainly the members of the gang of thugs must have withdrawn to some place; it should surely be possible to reconstruct the whole affair. Someone shouted: If the police really wanted to! Another: What had happened the night before was, from a political point of view, advantageous to the town. The authorities are against the measurements, and now they can say the population is also against the measurements; they, the population, showed with their fists that they were. Moreth: But that wasn't the population, last night. None of them were townspeople. Gasser, did you recognize any of the people last night? Gasser: No, he had not recognized anybody. Someone: But, also they weren't all—so he'd heard—from the Eisack valley. There were supposed to have been two or three Pakistanis among them. Perluttner: Pakistanis? The Pakistanis started a brawl here? Taschner: How did he know that they were Pakistanis? The other man: Perhaps there were also people of other nationalities there, perhaps he had only *assumed* that they were Pakistanis, they

are supposed to have looked like it. Someone: There are three Pakistanis working on Delazer's building, it could be them. Moreth: You
can't suspect people just because of the color of their skin. Perluttner:
Of course you can suspect people because of the color of their skin.
He had been suspect all his life because he was not an Italian. He was
a South Tyrolean. That had been suspicious from the start. His father
had opted for Hitler. Suspicious. Later, he, Perluttner, had not learned
Italian, and he always spoke German in the office. Suspicious. Then,
in the sixties, he had demonstrated on behalf of the Germanization of
the South Tyrol. More than suspicious. He landed in jail for that! And
now you're not allowed to be suspicious of a Pakistani, just because
he is a Pakistani? At this Perluttner certainly met with some violent
opposition. After a while, he himself conceded that the whole Eisack
valley was full of these idle Pakistanis, and Albanians and Muslims
as well; any one of them could be suspect, it didn't have to be the
three who worked for Delazer. In fact if you thought about it, Delazer
would have been foolish to have sent his own three Pakistanis, because no sooner had people heard of three Pakistanis than they
would all think of him immediately. At this very moment one of the
three Pakistanis suddenly appeared, out of the blue, in the Cellar.
Everyone stopped talking at once and looked at the man, almost in
fear. He sat down at the bar, ordered a beer, and drank it as fast as
possible; he apparently felt ill at ease as everyone was staring at him.
What's the matter? asked the Pakistani. Nothing was the matter, as
far as they were concerned, said someone. Was something the matter
with him? No, said the Pakistani surprised, why was he asking? I
just did, I just asked the question. You had to be allowed to ask a
question now and again, right? That's the way it is; if he came into

their land they were allowed to ask a question now and again. What do you mean *come* into their land? asked the Pakistani. He had been in Italy for ten years. First in Genoa, then in Asti, and now he was in Klausen. Perluttner: He had always been in Klausen. He had left Klausen only to defend his homeland, up at the fortress at the time. The Pakistani looked at him as though the old man were talking Chinese. Perluttner: We even landed in a concentration camp just because we didn't want to become Italian, in a concentration camp, Dachau, it's documented. Moreth: Whom do you mean by we? Perluttner: We, we sons of the fathers who opted against Italy. Moreth: You were in Dachau? Perluttner: No I wasn't in Dachau. But I could have landed there, it could have happened, it's documented, it's down in writing, the optants' sons were drafted and then if they did not serve they were sent to concentration camps. Moreth: The ones who opted for Italy were sent to Dachau, now you're confusing everything. You're talking about the book by Thaler. But Thaler opted for Italy, not for Hitler. Perluttner: He had read the book by Thaler, from cover to cover. He had not been an Italian, he was a small farmer, always German, and he was in Dachau, he, Perluttner, had read that himself. Moreth: Then read it again. Someone to the Pakistani: Where had he been last night? The Pakistani: Why was he asking him that? The other: Just asking. So where was he last night? The Pakistani: Where were you last night? The other man (confused): I . . . well I . . . I was at home, of course, I was at home, that is, I wasn't at home at first, I was . . . but it doesn't matter a bit where I was, that's not the question. Another man: After all, you're not a Pakistani. He: Yes, after all he wasn't a Pakistani. The Pakistani now looked much more frightened, although really the faces of the people there showed no sign of aggression; on the contrary, they reflected an absurd curiosity and an inquiring mind. People said, of course Huber can't say where he was last night, but ask his wife. Huber: Shut your trap, your filthy trap! The other: First he goes to Brixen, to the Brennerstrasse, then he goes somewhere up the hill to a meadow, to a meadow in the moonlight, there's nowhere more romantic to go with the ladies from the Brennerstrasse. Huber told the other man to shut up, and again the Pakistani did not understand a word; since he didn't have a car, he had never driven the ten kilometers to Brixen in the evening and had no idea about the Brennerstrasse, and so, of necessity, the conversation was, for him, completely baffling, especially as some of the members of the group had a heavy accent. He was asked again where he had been the night before and whether he had something to hide and so didn't want to say anything. He: He was, of course, at home. He had watched TV. And what, he was asked, had he watched? He: What he had watched? First, he said, he had watched the show about lawyers, then the news, then another feature movie, then half another movie . . . Another man: The usual evening format. The Pakistani: Yes, the usual evening format. Do you do something different in the evening? Everyone averted their eyes. Only Huber looked nervously at the wall and at his shoes. The Pakistani: Right, well I have answered your question and now you tell me why you're asking it! Aha, you don't want to say. Then I'll tell you. You're asking because of the brawl in the square in front of the school. People have spoken to me about that three times today already. First, it was said that there were no Klauseners there, but that the people had come from Villanders or Gufidaun, that's where the people had come from. Then it was said that there were no Eisack valley people there at all. But what people were they if they didn't come from the Eisack valley? Perluttner: Italians, of course, Italians! Why shouldn't it have been Italians? The Pakistani: He hadn't the faintest idea. Then, the third time, they suddenly wanted to know: What had he and his two colleagues actually been up to last night in the square in front of the school? And since then the Klauseners believe that they were there. Someone: The possibility that they were there could also not be excluded, or? He: The possibility that you were there could also not to be excluded, or? The other man: He was a South Tyrolean. That was different. The Pakistani now looked scared again, eyed the people—all of whose houses, in recent years, he had worked on, adding balconies or bay windows or repairing roofs, *et cetera*—quickly drank up, and left the pub. There's something wrong there, shouted somebody. Another man: What could the Pakistani have said other than what he did? The previous man: He himself would have said exactly the same. An alibi! The show about lawyers, the news, a full-length movie and then half of another movie. But then he should have had red eyes today after watching so much TV. Another man: You don't see that in their case, because of their color, because they are a completely different color from us. Perluttner: No one could watch as much TV as the foreigner claimed to have watched. Yes, someone said, one could, why yesterday evening he even saw the end of the show about lawyers, the news, *two* full-length movies, and a magazine program. Someone: Oh, a magazine program. He: A magazine program. A political magazine program! Badowsky, with a dirty laugh: Ha, a political magazine program at night! Frau Dr. Klein: She had also seen a political magazine program the night before. Her husband was asleep, for in spite of his sensitivity, he sleeps well, much better than she, she always had trouble getting to sleep, but he was sleeping, like a log, as always, so she turned on the TV. Moreth: And then your husband woke up again! She: No, he went on sleeping. Once he's asleep he sleeps. He also drinks a bottle of wine every evening. He drinks a tremendous amount. A bottle of wine every evening. At this, almost everyone in the front room of the Cellar stared blankly at the floor or at the opposite wall with as disinterested an expression as possible. Hm, a bottle of wine, that was . . . that was really a lot. Oh come on, someone shouted, you've already drunk that much at lunchtime. Someone: South Tyrolean wine is light, you could drink that. Another: Yes, wine, that's all part of it. *Et cetera, et cetera.* This conversation had a number of consequences. First of all, public opinion began to regard Gasser in a very critical light, because it was striking that he had said nothing about any of the issues that had been talked about and had expressed absolutely no opinion. This was not only seen as arrogant and presumptuous (". . . why is he standing around all the time and not saying anything?"), but it was also considered worrisome and even dangerous. To many of the people there, Gasser gave the impression of making observations, and of having had, for some time, a plan in mind, which was now coming more and more rapidly to fruition, and in a more and more threatening way, though it is true that no one could say what sort of plan it was and what its purpose was. Secondly, for whatever the reason might have been, it got around that Gasser did not support the citizens' action. But since it was considered absolutely impossible that he would be *against* it, people suspected a trick. Thirdly, it was recalled that Gasser was the brother of the woman to whom Martin Delazer was engaged and who intended to marry him in the near future. So there was a close tie between Josef Gasser and Martin Delazer! People began to spread rumors about this close tie. They began to wonder why Josef Gasser had so seldom been seen in public with Sonja Maretsch recently and why he kept on visiting the Piedmontese woman in Branzoll. Incidentally, it was rumored that Gasser was presently in a very aggressive mood, for it was said that, on the day before, in his mother's apartment, he had made a scene which had culminated in his forbidding his mother from reading magazines X and Y, in spite of the fact that probably at least seventy percent of all Klausen women were avid readers of these magazines. It was said of Gasser that he was anti-democratic. He was said to prefer an image of humanity—that he himself had created—to people themselves; he did not want to let people be themselves. People started to discuss whether something like right or wrong could be objectively possible. Is automobile traffic wrong *of itself*? No one seemed to find this *of itself* capable of substantiation. But if it could not be substantiated, then nothing could be derived from it. If the South Tyroleans wanted their roads and it could not *be objectively substantiated* that this was wrong, by what right could one dictate to the South Tyroleans what they could or could not do? After all, they were living in a democracy, where the concrete will of the majority, not the abstract truth of the individual, was supposed to prevail. (The latter was always arbitrary, while the will of the majority never was). Disputes of this sort actually went on in many places in Klausen, but admittedly not in these terms nor with this degree of clarity, but couched in the strongest dialect and with a thought structure that outsiders would scarcely have understood. People always talk in a way that assumes that other people think as they do, and they immediately blast the other person for being a fool if he does not understand their thought process, even though they do not, and never will, formulate this thought process, namely, because they are not in a position to do so. They are, rather, dependent upon the other person's having a related thought process; and when they think they have finally uncovered this related process in the other person, they say: Now you've finally got it, you ass, that's what I've been getting at all the time. In short: conversations that may scarcely be understood by the uninitiated, but which take place in a similar way all over the world—at least among ninety-five percent of the human race. Yet another consequence arose from the conversation in the front room of the Cellar. Gasser was charged with going to see his sister and asking her about the meaning of the previous night's events and also about Delazer's role in those events. So Gasser left the Cellar and started looking for his sister . . . at the time Katharina Gasser had a break from shooting her TV series and wanted to spend the time in Klausen. She was not living with her parents nor with her fiancé, Delazer, but in a hotel. The hotel was being paid for her by the production company. At the time, the production company paid for pretty much everything for Kati—her travel expenses were covered, so she always flew, to Munich, to Milan, to Rome (she always flew over the Eisack valley en route and looked at it from above: she recognized Brixen and Klausen every time); all her overnight stays were paid for; she received a per diem and so on; and, if she wished, they would also rent a car for her. So, in Klausen, she consistently stayed at the Goldener Elefant, the leading hotel on the town square, with a sauna, swimming pool, *et cetera*. Kati made use of both, the sauna as well as the swimming pool, and in fact it did seem to her that she was quickly getting regenerated, she was actually completely exhausted when she arrived in Klausen. But all the same her stay in her hometown turned out to be quite different from what she had imagined it would be. She had hardly to leave the hotel before finding herself in the midst of a commotion, and the commotion immediately fatigued her again, causing her to relapse into the jaded state in which she had arrived. Even in Klausen she could not go out alone. She always had a woman with her, provided by the production company, to keep the public at a distance, because of course everybody spoke to Kati. They all said the same things to her and asked her the same questions. What was it like to be famous? What was it like to be in films? And how did one handle success? Others, for example, asked her with great interest whether she would stay in the series— in which she played the colleague of a lawyer, played by X, the famous actor who, because he wanted to leave the series, had died in her arms the evening before—or would she also leave it now? The series, about which the Klauseners were very enthusiastic (they were constantly talking about it) had also become very well known in Austria and in Germany as well. It was said that the series, a co-production of two broadcasting organizations, was *a model for relations between the Burgenland and South Tyrol.* At the time, news broadcasts had even carried reports about the joint shoots, the governor's visit to the location, his conversation with the director, the screenplays were explained to the governor, the governor shook Kati Gasser's hand, *et cetera.* Of course, Kati was now asked by everyone on the streets of Klausen what it had been like working with X, the famous actor, how he had died in her arms, whether the kiss that he had given her as he lay dying in her arms was a real kiss (it looked as though it were), what were they to think about the kisses, whether there was a plan for a love affair with the new actor . . . why had there been no love affair with the old one . . . no love affair in a series, that was amazing, the expectation had always been that there would be a love affair in the end, but it had never come about . . . why? Didn't X want it? The questions went on and on like an endless circle. Kati was tired of listening to the questions, and so she had her colleague brush the nosy people aside. At this time Kati's appearances on the streets of Klausen were reminiscent of press conferences. Gasser caught up with his sister by the town hall. She was standing there in the midst of a crowd of people, cameras—from which came repeated flashes—held up over their heads, while her colleague was there with polite answers to any questions. Gasser remained standing somewhat apart, watching what was happening. Kati nodded, smiled, laughed, said two sentences, smiled again (all this had been rehearsed a hundred times), then her colleague raised both her hands, said the closing words of the press conference, and the two walked on and disappeared into Nussbaumer's. Gasser watched how the participants in the press conference remained in the street for a time. Many were delighted to see the famous actress—who had bought things in their shops as a child—back again in Klausen. One of them was a teacher and had taught Kati earlier in this or that subject, there was also someone with whom Kati was supposed to have been in the gym club, and they were all equally happy and enthusiastic. She was just the same, said some. She had completely changed, said others. After a while, a few people (in whom envy had suddenly gained the upper hand) said that she wasn't all that famous, a supporting role in actor X's lawyer show was not really fame, not in the real sense. Others:

But it was a meteoric rise. An old woman in an apron said that the Gasser girl can count herself lucky that X had also been in the show, for without X she would be unknown. A nothing. Besides she couldn't hold a candle to X. Not remotely. Anton Kerschbaumer from the Obergasse, the man who doted on Kati and had for months been collecting all the articles about Kati and especially all the photographs, got mad with the old woman in the apron, who obviously liked X. Kerschbaumer said that besides her TV activity, Miss Gasser had not only been in two full length movies (which, however none of those present in the street knew about) but, in a month's time, she would be in Rome playing the lead in a film directed by the famous director So and So. What was the film about? the people asked. Kerschbaumer: It was a love story, a love story set in the fifties . . . it was set, he believed, in England, as far as he knew. Wait a moment, no, he had recently read that it was set in Nice . . . not in England . . . but the film was mainly about Englishmen, he thought it also had something to do with the War . . . True, no one was listening to Kerschbaumer's confused statements, behind his back a few tapped their foreheads with their fingers, but in spite of this, his talk did make the majority consider Kati an established celebrity and one of the most important new actresses in the country. The participants in the press conference then broke up, and Gasser, who had been in the street listening to the whole discussion about his sister, went into Nussbaumer's. Kati was sitting there, with a female reporter, at a table that had been set aside from the others. Obviously she had an appointment for an interview. The reporter had placed a microphone on the table and was asking afresh all the same questions that Kati had just been asked in the street. The woman was from the Vorarlberg. The reporter's questions revolved primarily around one thing, which was obviously very important and of great interest to her: had it been X's wish that the kiss be written into the script, the final kiss, that he had given her, Katharina Gasser, last night while he was dying in her arms? Our female readers would naturally have found this scene deeply moving, said the Austrian woman, she had, she said, received many letters from readers beforehand, it was naturally always hard for our female readers to take leave of a character for whom they had felt such sympathy, like the one played by X. Gasser eyed his sister. Apparently Kati was somewhat strangely moved by the fact that this Austrian woman's female readership was only interested in X and his departure, but not in Katharina Gasser, the actress, and that, except for the kiss right at the end of the previous evening's final episode, she herself was completely out of the picture as far as this readership was concerned. Probably the whole female readership of the magazine envied Kati this one kiss, and that alone was the reason for today's interview. In any case, Kati said nothing to that effect, but, for her part, suddenly rattled on very enthusiastically about the female readership. She herself, she now maintained, had been able to sense from their reactions how *moved* the audience had been by the episode in question, the audience and hence the female readers of the magazine must have a very *fine feeling* for this and that; Kati praised the readership to the skies—for no reason, obviously this was simply part of the tone in which such interviews were conducted. Gasser watched the reporter. She was wearing a lemon-yellow suit and was sitting with her legs intertwined in a very cramped attitude, but always smiling and enthusiastic. She was virtually hanging on Kati's every word; on the other hand, she was apparently not paying attention to a single word and was not in the least interested in what Kati was saying. She somehow gave the impression of being nervous. She then said that of course she still needed a picture of Kati and had therefore commissioned a photographer from Bolzano who was, however, unfortunately (she looked at her watch) late, possibly stuck on the autobahn, the traffic was bad today. Yes, the traffic was bad, said Kati and she nodded, smiling. The microphone had meanwhile been switched off. At that moment, the photographer came into Nussbaumer's. Gasser took a step to one side. The photographer ran up to the Austrian, exchanged a few words with her, cast a quick glance at Kati, murmured a few words of greeting, and began to fuss with his camera. Meanwhile he was sizing up the room. Voices: Ah! Miss Gasser's being photographed! Make room, stand aside, she's going to be photographed! A photographer had arrived. Does anyone know the photographer? Some people said that the photographer had even photographed the governor. Everyone was impressed and watched what was happening. Wherever the photographer went everyone stood aside; the Klauseners yielded to celebrity like a plastic mass that gives way to the slightest pressure. In any case, the photographer was so hectically engaged in what he was doing that he was scarcely aware of it. He sat Kati on a chair, had her adopt two or three poses, then placed her in front of a wooden pillar, adjusted his camera a few times, even unfurled a screen, switched on a floodlight on a stand, and then sat down for a moment at an empty table, drank a glass of white wine mixed with water, staring the while into a complete void for about a minute, and then got up again. All the Klauseners who were at Nussbaumer's were very impressed by the photographer's feverishness. From one appointment to the next, he gave them the impression of absolute importance. I couldn't live like that, someone said. But after all we're only Klauseners, said someone else. While this was going on, a few Klauseners were looking thoughtfully at Katharina Gasser. Meantime, the latter and her assistant were standing around with the Austrian woman for a moment longer. All three of them were congratulating each other and expressing their pleasure at the meeting, for usually—all three of them said—these appointments were always a bit . . . how shall I put it? . . . but this one had given them all great pleasure, *et cetera*. After this the reporter left Nussbaumer's and so terminated Katharina Gasser's appointment. Gasser, who had been standing at the bar for a long time, now sat down by his sister. Kati's colleague immediately got up and was about to get rid of him, but Kati told the woman that this was her brother. Her colleague begged her pardon and introduced herself as Signora Finozzi. After a short, general conversation with Kati and Finozzi, Gasser introduced his request or, to put it better, the request of those people who had previously been sitting in the bar of the Cellar. He inquired about Delazer's participation in the previous night's happenings. Kati looked at him questioningly and wanted to know what happenings he was talking about. She claimed to know nothing about what had happened on the previous night. Gasser now explained things in detail to her. Among other things Kati learned from him in detail for the first time, were all the particulars of Taschner and his action, and that Sonja's brother had been beaten up—this she found particularly horrible, because she liked Christian Maretsch, and had known him from before. Signora Finozzi also appeared shocked at the occurrences as they were reported and could not believe that such things could happen in a town like Klausen, in the heart of the provinces, in the idyllic Eisack valley. Gasser could see that the local clientele in Nussbaumer's, who looked upon Finozzi with unparalleled respect, were also looking at him with a strange look—since he had been sitting at the table—as though he belonged to a circle of the absolutely elect. No one, it was clear to Gasser, would now dare to sit at their table (a year before anyone would not have hesitated to sit at a table with Katharina Gasser, if they had seen any reason to do so). And, in truth, everyone knew Gasser was Kati's brother, but still their respect for him increased abruptly just because he was sitting with his sister and the unapproachable Finozzi. The way the Klauseners suddenly kept their distance from him disgusted Gasser. Kati seemed somewhat affected by the rumor that, in the course of the whole ugly affair of the previous night, Martin Delazer was said to have appeared in the square in front of the old school as one of the gang around Laner, who, as she said, she did not like. She said that she had often been to Laner's house, but that since Laner's stretch in jail she found everything to do with him and everything connected with him suspect. For this reason she could not say what Martin had wanted in the square last night, but he could ask him himself straightaway, for they were meeting here at one o'clock. It was almost one. Gasser decided to stay, although he did not like Delazer. Delazer arrived and shrugged off all the questions he was asked and said nothing about the previous night, but spoke most good humouredly about something quite different that was occupying him, namely, Laner's quarrels with a certain Alois Zurner in Brixen. Three weeks later Delazer said that Gasser had shown great interest in what he was saying at the time, but from the outset he could not believe that Gasser should have come after him as the agent of the Cellar group, and he was sure Gasser had done it on his own account and in his own interest. He had tried to sound him out, to find out what he was after. Possibly he, Delazer, had thought at first that Gasser was doing it for Taschner or Maretsch, but later he no longer thought that, because Gasser's interest in the citizens' action group was probably only a pretence, a camouflage. So, on that occasion at Nussbaumer's, he, Delazer, had talked about something quite different, about the quarrel between Laner and Zurner, but he had certainly not foreseen what he was starting by telling the story in such detail. The quarrel arose over a real-estate conflict. Delazer related the whole business, perhaps simply because he liked to pretend that he was aware not only of everything that was happening in the economy of the Eisack valley, but also that *he had his finger in every pie and that nothing at all could happen without his being involved* (incidentally, he was always cementing his position in the South Tyrolean provincial parliament by exactly this sort of performance, and he did it without ever having been taught how to act like this in a seminar on rhetoric—he did it entirely thanks to his magnificent instincts). A year before, Zurner had bought a parcel of land on the Eisack, above the Brixen industrial park. The purchase would not have attracted any further attention, if it had not been that Laner, the Minister for Agriculture, had previously acquired the surrounding parcels. At the time, Laner had tried to get permission to build a housing development; the buildings had already been planned by Delazer's office, models were being built: two and three-room apartments in buildings that each contained ten units. At the time, Zurner was still a completely unknown realtor, but he had already begun to invest, here and there, in undertakings of his own. He had bought a building that had been scheduled for demolition, together with the land around it, in the center of Brixen, but had kept the building, rehabilitated it with the help of public money, and installed a cinema complex inside it. He had then leased this out. As a second enterprise he had enlarged a building into a discotheque called *Sam*, he operated the Sam himself. As result of all this, Zurner had become a person who played a certain role in the Brixen town council and who had contacts, at the least in Brixen, and, as is well known in politics and in free enterprise, there is nothing more important than good contacts. There was a story behind the purchase on the bank of the Eisack. The parcel Zurner had bought lay plumb in the middle of the housing development planned by Laner. Thus Zurner not only owned the parcel through which the approach road had to run, but at the same time he held in his hands the prime piece of the whole proposed complex. Gasser listened with great interest to Delazer's explanation and could picture the whole situation. He asked the architect why Laner had not bought this parcel as well. The call for bids on the project had presumably only been made after Laner had already completed the plans and had already acquired his parcels. Delazer replied that that unfortunately was not the whole story. The building authorities should have worked more closely with them, they should have been more closely attuned to the project, above all, it should not be thought that the seller was so naïve as not to have sniffed out why Laner should suddenly have become interested in these utterly remote and unimportant parcels of land. Gasser asked once more why a man like Laner didn't immediately purchase the parcel which now belonged to Zurner. Delazer: He wasn't able to say why precisely. First of all there was something about some leases, the old Ploder castle was situated on the land and at the moment people are living in it, foreigners, Moroccans and Albanians and so forth. Zurner is not stupid, he knows what it means to have those foreigners there. If you put people like that into your property today, it's true that you have no income, but the Office for the Preservation of Historical Monuments can also not touch you, because these foreigners—who are all of course unemployed—are sacrosanct, nothing happens if they are established in the buildings in question. As I say, Zurner is not stupid. Gasser: Just a moment. Did you say that we were talking about the parcel with Ploder castle on it? Delazer: Yes, Ploder castle. Gasser: Do you mean to say that a development has been approved for where Ploder castle stands? Delazer: First of all, he did not know what, where, who, or how anything had been approved, that was entirely Zurner's business, because the castle belongs to him, and secondly, what for God's sake was anyone going to do with that old heap? The ruins were on the brink of collapsing. He himself had inspected it. It was absolutely impossible for anyone to do anything with it . . . Delazer went on talking about the building for a while. He told lies, obfuscated the issue, and got entangled in this and that contradiction, but he said everything with great emphasis, as though the whole matter were a provincial farce with Zurner as the driving force. According to his account, Laner was completely in the right, although, as was clear from the same account, Laner must have brought the whole authority responsible for the project into disrepute. And Delazer admitted, on the one hand, that he had drawn up the building plans, as Laner's representative, he himself had had them approved, but then again, he said he had no idea what, how, where or when anything had been approved, et cetera. It became clear to Gasser that Laner had simply wanted to demolish Ploder castle. The castle was, of course, the reason why, up till then, no one had been interested in the parcel, because the purchaser would have been stuck with the castle and would have had to invest incredible sums of money in it. All of this, it is true, was very confusing in the small print but, overall, quite straightforward, and Gasser was surprised that Delazer was so outspoken about the matter in public. How has the matter been resolved then? he asked Delazer. Delazer said that absolutely nothing had been resolved. The two antagonists were now dutifully carrying on their quarrel in the newspapers. Recently Zurner had even been distributing flyers on the cathedral square in Brixen; these flyers were designed to explain to the citizens of Brixen how important Zurner's project was for the town and that he was only doing it all for charitable reasons. Gasser: what sort of project? What project did this man Zurner have in mind? Delazer: Zurner maintains, for his part, that he wants to build there. He calls the project *Living in Brixen*. He has commissioned an architectural firm to draw up the plans, but he, Delazer, is of the opinion that Zurner merely wants to force up the price of the Ploder castle parcel. Because what he, Delazer, believed was that, in the long run, Zurner wanted to sell to Laner and that he had only bought the parcel so that it would double or triple in price. Delazer looked at the two women who, because of what he was saying, were staring at him more or less open-mouthed, either because what they were hearing was absolutely scandalous or they simply didn't understand it and therefore found it utterly boring . . . Gasser then went walking through the streets for a while, reflecting on this meeting at Nussbaumer's. Above all he was thinking about what Delazer had told him about Zurner and Ploder castle. Auer had also spoken to him recently about the castle, for he had often been in the building. He had been drinking with some of the Moroccans or Albanians and had stayed in the castle for a few days. He had spent the night there and had not left the castle during the days mentioned; he had sat around in the garden with the Moroccans or Albanians (perhaps also with people of quite different nationalities, or with Badowsky), and they had barbequed an ox and must have been drinking prodigiously, in any case Auer had not been very forthcoming about the stay. But he had told him that they had been shooting at bottles with a rifle. But that was possibly not true, for Auer frequently invented such stories or, at least, exaggerated them beyond all measure. Auer had also talked about a damp mattress, a roof that had collapsed, and about being so drunk that he had locked himself in a toilet for half a day—he wasn't able to let himself out—but Gasser did not know either what Auer was really after in the castle, nor with whom he came into contact there. Gasser intended to ask Auer about it. He suddenly had an almost insatiable interest in visiting Ploder castle as soon as possible, in being introduced to, and getting to know, the people . . . Gasser went into some pub, asked for some writing paper, and wrote down everything Delazer had told him about the castle and about Zurner—word for word as far as possible. He wrote five pages, put them into his overcoat, and then went to the Cellar and looked through the last three days' *Eisacktaler Tagblatt*, but he could only find one single article that had anything to do with Zurner, and that only marginally. That is to say, Zurner himself was not even mentioned in the article but only his discotheque, the Sam (Sam apparently had no significance other than that it was an Anglo-American given name). Gasser read the article most attentively, in spite of its marginal relevance. The article had a report on the South Tyrolean Society for the Protection of Birds, which had furnished the municipality of Brixen with an expert opinion on the catastrophic effect of the searchlight on Sam's discotheque upon migratory birds. Gasser tore the article out and put it into his pocket as well. He then went to the office of the Tourist Association and worked for the whole of the rest of the day. He spent the whole time there, after first moving his chair behind a partition, so as not to be seen, resting his feet on the bookshelf opposite him, and, in this manner, reflecting on all sorts of things. In time he became so exhausted by reflecting like this that he would have almost fallen asleep, if various tourists had not kept appearing to inquire about the most varied things—as they did every day. Auer too appeared at some point and sat down behind the partition with him for an hour, and there they sat smoking and drinking. Every time any tourists came through the glass door into the office, Gasser would remove his feet from the shelf with concentrated dilatoriness, tidy himself up, and take his place behind the counter. He answered all the questions he was asked with perfect sovereignty, as he did every day, although of late he had adopted the habit of misleading—in a really crazy way—people who wanted certain information. He sent them all over the place, mostly south on the autobahn, and told them not to leave the autobahn until they had reached Trento. (Almost all of them followed these instructions dutifully). Three Italians looking for a hotel were the first to arrive in the Tourist Association when Auer was there; then a few Upper Italian adolescents came into the office, apparently on a school excursion, and they obviously thought it would be a joke to inquire about a pizzeria; and then a few Germans came in. When German tourists come into the Tourist Association in Klausen they are always in the same age group, that is, they are pensioners, and they always come exclusively as a pair if they are not in a group. Even their clothes are often stereotypical in a ghastly way. They often wear knickerbockers and red or green knee-length socks and, in addition, they have caps on their heads: men and women only differ in that the man goes ahead and asks the questions while the woman stands behind him, rummaging through all the municipal advertising brochures, bringing them into total disarray, and then asks the man—impatiently and almost spitefully—what he has finally found out. Gasser told them that the town was fully booked and that they would not be able to find even a single room in any hotel; as support for his statement, he invented a medical convention that was taking place in Klausen at this time—as it always did annually during these particular weeks—and because of which Klausen was filled to capacity. There was simply nothing to be done for them in Klausen at the moment, the best thing, he told the tourists, would be to go to Bolzano or, even better, to Trento, in Trento he knew for sure that there were still vacant rooms, good rooms, good and not expensive. Yes, Trento, but . . . do they speak German in Trento? Gasser said that people didn't even speak German in Klausen any longer. German was only spoken in the Tourist Association in Klausen, even the menus in Klausen were in Italian. Upon which the Germans hastily left town and Gasser and Auer had their fun. That evening, a largish group got together: Gasser, Badowsky, Auer, Zanetti, *et cetera*. They first visited several bars, and then they all went up to Brixen, to Ploder castle, and spent the night there. Gasser did not turn up for work the next day. This day, and the following night, soon became legendary in Klausen. Rumors spread about the most diverse things, everything was described in the most glowing colors: it was said that the group around Gasser did not return to Klausen until the second night, when they had all gone straight to the Cellar and drunk incredible amounts. Badowsky is supposed to have shouted insanely that it was the greatest party he had ever seen; mind you, he was still thought not to have a penny in his pocket—where the money came from that they all spent on drink, no one could say. Zanetti, apparently, spent half the night going on about the law of economics, and then, after he had climbed onto a table, is supposed to have given a lecture on the *Second Law of Thermodynamics*—incidentally, the lecture was completely incomprehensible, no one had any idea how he had hit upon the topic, and he kept on clapping his hands. All this and the strange elation that permeated the whole drunken group is supposed to have been a complete puzzle to those who witnessed it. Everyone was talking about it the next day, but with wildly different versions of what had happened. And now things began to move faster and faster until they finally stopped. On the following morning, Gasser had, in fact, disappeared; there was nothing of his to be seen, except for his overcoat, which he had left behind in the Cellar (for the simple reason, it was supposed, that he had been too drunk to remember to take it). Auer was called upon by the police that same morning and taken to the station, and Badowsky escaped the clutches of the police by running into a bar, storming into the wash-rooms, leaving the building by the back window, jumping into the Eisack, and bidding farewell to Klausen for the next few days. It was then learned that the following events had taken place in Brixen during the night: Around 10:30 P.M., Alois Zurner had come out of a bar in the Albuingasse, where he was a regular customer, and where he had gone to have a drink with his

partners—in a relaxed atmosphere (that's what he called it)—to cel-
ebrate their business transactions. He had been in the bar with a
businessman from Sterzing, had drunk five half liters of red wine
with him, and then called a cab for him. Zurner himself was on foot,
walking first across the cathedral square and then through the street,
the so-called *Stinkergass*—which, as always, stank of cheese—past
the Finsterwirt.[2] There, he met an acquaintance; they were both
upset by the smell, which had for decades been just as popular a subject of conversation on that particular street, as the weather was elsewhere. His acquaintance then said that Zurner should eject the cheese
monger. Zurner said, But where would his wife buy her goat cheese?
In the whole of Brixen, goat cheese was still only to be had in a single
shop, which was run, of all things, by Italians. After chatting for
five minutes about the Italians and their place in the South Tyrolean
economy, Zurner walked on. He now left the old city area and turned
south, for Zurner lived in a large house in the Spaur-strasse. There is
a wall behind the palace with a small gateway in it that almost no one
in Brixen knows about—no one pays any attention to it because it is
always closed by an age-old wooden door that's barely six feet high.
Zurner was standing in front of this gateway, puzzled, and, because
it was standing open, he noticed it for the first time in his life. He
looked in, and he saw some espalier fruit trees, an herb garden, and
gardening tools; everything lay in a bright light because the historical walls of the palace above the espalier were lit by strong flood-
lights. Standing there in the archway (Zurner is a normal South
Tyrolean, and so, without having to bend down, fits under a lintel

---

2. An old established hotel in Brixen.

that is just under six feet in height), he was undecided whether he should go into the little garden, which he thought looked most charming, or whether he should inform someone and let them know that the gateway was open and should be shut, simply for the sake of good order. Zurner also saw a cross on a small altar that was standing bathed in a delightful light, and he felt an impulse—without any more urging and simply as a result of his Catholic upbringing—to kneel down and say the Lord's Prayer. Anyway, at that moment, he received a shove from behind and found himself in the little garden. He was thrown to the ground, heard the door close, and was, as he quickly realized, completely helpless. As everything had gone black, he at first saw nothing, and he also made no move to try to see anything, because his head had been rammed face down into the earth and at the same time he was being kicked in the side, so that he thought he was sure to die that instant. Then his arm was twisted and someone knelt on his back, but, strangely enough, no one went for his wallet, all he heard was mocking laughter. The abuses now heaped upon Zurner were numerous and particularly vicious; Zurner did not recognize anyone, and the voices he heard all sounded South Tyrolean, from the Eisack valley, perhaps, he later stated, that he had also heard one from Bolzano and from the Puster valley but certainly an Italian. The Italian had kept shouting *porco dio, dio bestia* whenever he kicked him. In this difficult situation, Zurner, who was being pinned to the ground, conversed with some of his assailants. Zurner wanted to know—and he had enough courage and sense to ask this— what it was that they wanted of him and why they were treating him so cruelly. He would have expected all sorts of things, above all he would have expected that they would say he should immediately and unconditionally, and at a decent price, sell the Ploder castle lot to Laner, for otherwise he would never have another day's peace on this earth, *et cetera*, but strangely enough they never said a word about this, instead they said something about birds and lights, and at first Zurner didn't have the faintest idea what they were talking about. They mocked him all the more for this, kicked him harder, and, worse than that, they twisted one of his ears so that he almost had to cry out (he was taking care not to cry out, for that would have been the worst thing he could have done at that moment). So, someone said, now he could see what we should do to all of them. Which all are you talking about? said Zurner, groaning as they went on kicking. All those who sweep the sky with their beams just for the sake of profit. Keep the skies free, someone shouted; Exactly! cried another one, keep the skies free at last. Zurner: But the searchlight has been approved. Still more kicks, his ear was twisted more fiercely, it really seemed as though it would be torn off. We're finishing off people of your caliber one after the other, everyone. Leave the birds in peace, leave our eyes in peace, leave the sky in peace, now, you're to leave everything in peace. Do you understand, you pig! At least two of them burst into laughter at this; they obviously thought the whole business very amusing and did not take it really seriously. But you can't torture a man like this just because you have something against the searchlight, cried Zurner. I'm a businessman. At this someone kicked him on the head, apparently as punishment for the word *searchlight* or the word *businessman*. You filthy pig! cried someone. You Antichrist! cried another. People came flailing at him so violently that Zurner began to say the Lord's Prayer and fainted as he did so. When he came to, a few hours later, still in the same beautifully lit garden (the gate was closed), he discovered that he was almost in no state to move. It was only after a quarter of an hour that he was able to stand up. He saw that there were papers lying on the ground round about him, they looked like flyers. Zurner tried to read one of them but he couldn't, he was still too dizzy. Then, he did manage to after all. The flyer contained threats against people who shined searchlights into the sky or did all sorts of other things (cut down mixed forests, built golf-courses), and there was a longish excursus about migratory birds. The flyer ended like this: *An end to the acceptance of baseless actions.* No author's name appeared on the flyer. It was some time before Zurner could get out of the garden, and then he dragged himself to the police station and from there he was taken to the hospital. Different opinions were expressed about the incident even in Klausen. A few people said, quite openly, that there was nothing more unnecessary and pointless than illuminating the whole sky over the Eisack valley—as though there were a war on—just for the sake of a discotheque. That's megalomania, said Klein, and the new hedonism's affectation of power. Others too considered (and this was indeed the case) these fingers of light useless and harmful, and people were annoyed with the town of Brixen for allowing this pitiable spectacle to take place four times a week, week after week. But if the one town did it, then the other one would too, in order to remain competitive, and so everything would take its course and ultimately what the towns were mainly interested in was their income and tourism, *et cetera.* That's the way things are: Actually these fingers of light were more pointless and (for the birds) more dangerous than anything else, but no one could prevent them. That's what they call progress, someone shouted. Others compared it with the heavy freight-vehicle traffic on the Brenner autobahn. That too could not be stopped, also for reasons of competition. If one firm did it, then the other would do it too. If you want peace, shouted Perluttner several times that day, then prepare for war. People recognized that Perluttner's statement bore a resemblance to the thought that had been expressed—that what one did the other would also do—and so you have be the first to do it because, in any event, the other would not refrain from doing it himself. And so humanity can always be said to be forcing itself along the path of progress just by following the stated maxim. Many, of course, found it scandalous and quite inappropriate that Zurner had been so badly treated simply because of his searchlight (the people who came to Brixen regularly to go to Sam's were terribly perturbed, they couldn't understand the facts of the case at all, they couldn't see anything wrong with the searchlight: they found it exceptionally pleasing; they always found Brixen much more attractive when the searchlight was switched on than at other times and, as a whole, they felt less bored and disoriented when they looked at the town). Others, on the other hand, quite openly experienced a certain malicious glee. They didn't care, one way or the other, why Zurner had been treated the way he was, the main thing was that he'd been treated that way, that's what pleased them. A few men, they said, had finally plucked up some courage and shown *those people* that they could not simply do what they were doing, *et cetera*. It appeared that a lot of the townspeople could suddenly conjure up a heap of resentment against everything that had to do with money, the economy or politics. Of course, whether they were motivated by good sense or envy is open to question. The morning after the attack, a police car drove up to Ploder castle. An entry was forced. Since no one would open up—apparently the police contingent had been anxiously observed from the windows—the police opened the door themselves (it was not locked) and looked for the first available people to speak to, and all the Moroccans and Albanians were terribly confused, did not seem to understand anything, and retreated into the remotest parts of the castle. There were even a few Kurds in the castle. The police looked with disgust at a heap of a hundred beer and schnapps bottles standing in one corner of the courtyard. Who put that there? they asked. An Albanian family looked helplessly at it and quickly disappeared. A Moroccan was sorting through the pile of bottles for any dregs that could still be drunk. There was something picturesque about the scene. The Brixen public had no knowledge of the exact state of affairs in Ploder castle, people had long been forced to rely on rumor alone and a lot of tales were told. But what had been said about conditions in Ploder castle now seemed not only to be confirmed but even to have been exceeded by the truth, for whenever a rumor is confirmed, the truth ultimately seems more grotesque than the rumor. The police questioned the residents, by turns, for more than an hour, but everything proceeded very chaotically. The Moroccans and the Albanians, for their part, had a mortal fear of the Brixen police, and the Brixen police found this completely incomprehensible. An Albanian woman wearing a headscarf spread her hands out, palm upwards, to the police, pleaded, and, with tears in her eyes, shouted out a few phrases in Albanian. No one understood what she was saying. The policeman did not even understand the gesture; he did not know what it meant when someone (an Albanian woman) turns the palms of her hands up and spreads them out, because he had never seen anything like it before. A Moroccan even climbed up the wall of the castle, in order to jump into a hayrick on the other side from which he could escape, and the police were vainly shouting at him that all they wanted were the answers to a few questions. The police finally received the following answers to their questions. Yesterday there had been a great crowd of Germans, or at least German-speakers, here. Among the crowd was a Marcus Badowsky and a Leopold Auer, the latter was reputedly a writer who came from Klausen, was well-known there, and often came to drink—he talked to them a lot, but never had any money. The other was a scrounger who had turned up there four weeks before, he had had a girl with him at first—a very young girl by the way—who, after a while and several quarrels, had left him. The police received a detailed description of how the crowd had behaved: it seemed that they had spent almost two days drinking and that the last ones had finally disappeared, or gone to bed, late at night on the second day. Whereupon Auer was questioned. Since he was drunk he was unable to remember anything. In any case, he uttered—with great verve—insults against any number of different people. For example, he described Zurner many times as *a capitalist*. The police also asked about Zurner's searchlight and what Auer thought about it. Auer said that Zurner should of course be punished for the searchlight. After this, Auer was provisionally arrested. In his advanced state of intoxication he also mentioned a few other names, Gasser's among them. Finally, however, it turned out that, at the time of the attack, Auer had been sitting for several hours on a wooden bench not far from the castle teaching a young Albanian girl two chords on the guitar and teaching her, by means of these two chords, the Italian National Anthem (or at least the beginning of it); in fact, the residents had complained of a breach of the peace and sent for a police car—it was hard to think of a better alibi. And so Auer was let go again. Zanetti had left the next day for a meeting in Pisa and only came back two days later. He went at once to the police station and made the following statement: A large crowd, he said, had gathered at Ploder castle on the night in question. Certainly fifteen or twenty people, who had come from all over the place, had sat round a fire, including a few leftist Germans, two Carinthian anti-fascists (they were said to have kept on referring to themselves as *Carinthian anti-fascists* but no one could understand why; they had been rather aggressive and had spoken very salaciously about the young Albanian girls who were present in the castle), a few Italians who were very sun-tanned, and he, Zanetti, had gotten the impression that they were building workers; in response to a question by the police, Zanetti also stated that yes, it was possible that there had also been Pakistanis in the crowd, possibly three, but he had not been able to make them out properly by the light of the fire. He went on to say that on the evening in question he had had a bitter quarrel with Gasser and that the two of them had not exchanged a single word since, not even later on in Klausen after they had returned there. The crowds that had collected at Ploder castle seemed to him, Zanetti, to have consisted in large part of people who were passing through on their way to a demonstration or some other political event, but he had not been able to figure it out properly—a great deal of alcohol had been consumed, and furthermore, because of his quarrel with Josef Gasser, he had not been concentrating. Zanetti could not, or would not, make a clear statement about the cause of the quarrel. He also said that, in the course of the evening, the group had already partly split up, only to gather around the fire again later in a somewhat different configuration; the composition of the crowd assembled there had fluctuated wildly, he himself, for example, had soon lost sight of Auer and, later on, Gasser, at least from time to time. He said that, in the course of the evening, Badowsky, with the two Carinthians and another person, had forced his way into the apartment of one of the Albanian families, looking for schnapps or looking for a girl, and created a disturbance there; he, Zanetti, at least—and others as well—had, after a few hours, found things getting too out of hand and too outrageous (even the songs that were being sung were outrageous, he said), and when Gasser reappeared they all went back to Klausen. Unfortunately the evil-smelling and totally objectionable Badowsky had latched on to them and also returned to Klausen with them, *et cetera*. Of course, the night in Ploder castle assumed a quite story-like stature throughout Klausen. Gasser was made out to be part violent criminal, part hero of the resistance. On the other hand, several people saw in Zanetti a calumnious and vicious character, a sort of Mephisto spreading his poison among people, while others considered the Florentine university assistant the only decent and sober-minded person in the whole heap of wickedness and abomination that had gathered around people like Gasser and Auer. Gasser, people said, had gone back to Berlin, making a sort of tactical withdrawal, he had enough contacts there, *et cetera*. But for days the talk in Klausen was all about the Moroccans, the Albanians, and especially conditions in Ploder castle. What was remarkable, though, was the following: Perluttner suddenly began singing all kinds of songs about Andreas Hofer—in the street and in pubs—and when the talk turned to Gasser's son, there was a strange glint in his eyes—an absolutely light blue glint—they had completely

regained their youthful appearance, as though it were fifty years earlier. One could have thought that the public was nothing but a form
of madness. But how rapidly all sorts of people yielded to the complete lack of restraint (and, in the process, felt themselves to be mere
recipients of information)! At certain moments, Gasser was clearly
portrayed to the point of caricature, but the picture revealed strange
lacunae. Later, after the whole catastrophe at the bridge had actually
taken place, Gasser was even said to have been involved in planning
an attempt on Delazer's life, using the rifle, which has already been
mentioned, and, it was said, he had only planned the attempt because,
out of jealousy of his sister, he detested Delazer heartily, even to the
point of hatred. At first no one was bothered that no shot had ever
been fired and no rifle was ever found; in fact, the papers printed
pictures of the parcel that had been found near the lime silo and were
puzzled as to why Gasser had not ultimately carried out the attack.
Gasser eventually became the worst sort of Hofer. But back to the
events. A few days after the earlier events, a strange leaflet turned
up. This leaflet was displayed in various places overnight and had
also been posted up as a placard on various exterior walls. At the
same time, the identical text could be viewed on the web page of the
Klausen Tourist Association; this was curious, someone had obviously hacked into the page. Gruber and young Moreth—they were
actually part of a large crowd—happened to read the placard at about
half past nine in the morning on an exterior wall next to Nussbaumer's. Pamphlets like this one—on all sorts of topics—could recently
be seen with ever increasing frequency, and, for some time, these generally anonymous statements contained a clearly inherent tendency to
escalate, because over the whole of Europe the attitudes expressed in

these papers had recently grown more and more extreme, more angry, and more full of hatred. A few people in front of Nussbaumer's
slapped their thighs delightedly as they read the placard and pointed
out to one another what they thought were especially well-chosen
expressions. Others looked blankly at the placard, immediately flew
into a rage, and turned red in the face, because it seemed to them that
what they were reading was a great insult to Klausen. Gasser's name
soon came up. Actually, however, the whole thing was signed with
an *A*. That could be an abbreviation for *anonymous* or, of course, it
could mean something quite different. All that could be said with
certainty was that the placard could not reflect the views of the Klausener authorities. And, as became apparent in several conversations
on the following day, and already that same evening, in all the nooks
and crannies of this town, that was studded with nooks and crannies,
the pamphlet in no way reflected the thinking of the large majority
of Klauseners, who, for the most part, did not understand a word of
it; what the anonymous *A* had written seemed to them completely
mistaken. In his pamphlet, the anonymous author had denigrated
Klausen and its inhabitants. He declared that the town and the province had ruined virtually everything in the valley. In the course of a
few decades, the old town of Klausen had expanded on all sides and
up into the hills with ever larger and more grotesque buildings. (The
anonymous author repeatedly used the word *workplaces* without plac-
ing it in any context and always—with his strange logic—as a syno-
nym for destruction, demolition or, quite simply, ugly buildings. All
this was written in a very derisive tone.) Workplaces! cried Gruber in
the midst of the crowd, clapping his hands in rapture. Continuing *A*:
The hillside opposite—scratched out like a wound (that was where

the limestone was quarried). The Eisack—divided by a multi-stage system of dams, its banks dead straight, strengthened with concrete. The river was crossed by bridges, bridges that were almost slabs up by the entrance to the autobahn, village-sized slabs (that is the word he used). Under these slab bridges—nothing but darkness. Above the silo, the autobahn bridge, the A22, supported by gigantic reinforced concrete pillars that rammed into the woods and the hillside. The autobahn snakes its way like a dragon through the valley and buries everything beneath it left and right. Every now and again, the autobahn itself rams into the side of the hill, ten kilometers downstream they have tunneled under the old Trostburg, *et cetera*, and the text went on and on in this tone saying that, a few hundred meters to the north, the autobahn branches into a tangled network that occupies the whole right-hand side of the valley: the toll booth, the entrance, the exit to Klausen, the road to Gufidaun, the other road to X all covered by a string of street lamps and signs. The roads surround the old farmhouses like nooses that are drawn tighter from one development scheme to the next. A lot of people have long since moved away, their houses razed. The noise in the valley was colossal, wrote the anonymous author. (A few people in front of Nussbaumer's immediately agreed; it even seemed to them that the anonymous writer was simply giving a very detailed description of the state of affairs. But nevertheless they also said that the anonymous writer, just because of the great attention to detail, must have a total pathological fixation.) And further: Side by side with the dam, the giant bacon factory complex. Next door to this the equally gigantic Eisack valley winery. The two complexes, almost as large as the whole of the old town of Klausen. *Et cetera*. A few people in the crowd standing in front of the wall where the placard was posted began a heated conversation. Soon they all went into Nussbaumer's, followed by Gruber and Moreth. Giuseppe Neri was sitting at a table and gesticulating excitedly with his right hand, as he talked to, or argued with, Alderman Valli. The Communists, that's what they always say, the Communists! cried Neri; he was almost shouting and was constantly interrupting in Italian. What about the Communists? What have the Communists ever done in Italy? They've never done anything, nothing. Italians never do anything at all. That's Italy all over, Italy does nothing. Even the fascists, what did they do, the Italian fascists? We had Rome, Rome was great, in the old days, but the fascists weren't. Valli: But they did have Mussolini, the undemocratic system . . . futurism. Neri: Huh! That wasn't what he was talking about. Mussolini and? And beyond that? Mussolini, what was that supposed to mean? That's nothing but your arguments, I'm not going to listen to them, it doesn't interest me. Keep on fighting with your Gassers and so on, but leave us in peace. Hanspaul Meraner was sitting at a table drinking a Waldler[3] and said, completely relaxed, that they hadn't needed to come there. Now Neri lost his cool. He jumped up, gesticulated even more violently with his right hand, and shouted, Whom did he mean by *you*, tell them! Tell them at once whom he meant by *you*. Meraner: You Italians, that's who I mean. Ah, cried Neri. You Italians! But have you looked at your passport, have you? And what does that say? Italian that's what it says. Meraner: He didn't give a damn what his passport said. That had been ridiculous from the word go. At least they don't incarcerate us any more whenever we say what

---

3. A raspberry liqueur peculiar to South Tyrol.

I've just been saying—the Italians don't. Neri was now standing in the middle of the room and was using both arms in a gesture which would not have had such a tremendous effect in the south as it did here in Klausen. I don't need South Tyrol! he cried. You can do what you like. You don't want me? Good! Then I'll just go away again. Do you think for one moment it was my own idea to come here. I'm only human too. I was told, go to Alto Adige, there's work there, that's where the economy is growing, they said. And then I thought, that's Italy. I simply thought, that's Italy. Valli: But it is Italy. Don't dramatize everything so! We've long since solved all these problems. Meraner: We haven't solved anything. It says in my passport that I come from Tecelinga, but I don't come from Tecelinga, I come from Töt-schling, I don't know any Tecelinga. Just because some fascist scholar invented the name Tecelinga, I'm far from coming from Tecelinga; Meraner had beads of perspiration on his forehead. He too was now standing in the middle of the room, ten feet away from Giuseppe Neri. I can tell you precisely why I do not come from Tecelinga, Neri! he cried. And why, why not! shouted Neri and threw up his hand. Meraner: Because I come from Tötschling. Neri cried that he did not need Tecelinga, he was not the Italian state, he had not brought about the state of affairs, he was not responsible for anything at all. Or is it perhaps my fault, he cried, that I was told to come here, is it my fault that I saw that damned vacancy advertized in the paper and applied for it? Meraner stood trembling in the middle of the room and could not find an answer. Neri sat down, and then Meraner followed suit. Just imagine, he said turning once more to Neri. What? asked Neri and drank a glass of red wine in one gulp. Meraner: Just imagine, you are living in a village now and you learn that in four weeks time it will have a new name, your village's new name. And for four weeks the villagers stand around smirking at one another and coming up with all sorts of different ideas, and then comes the news. Tötschling is to become Tecelinga. Tötschling is wiped off the map and in its place there is now Tecelinga, although there is, of course, not a single Italian resident in Tötschling, which no longer exists, and which is suddenly called Tecelinga. The first Italian came to Tecelinga in 1984, as a tourist, but that was forty years after the name had been changed. After the fascists had renamed it. First of all, everyone is splitting their sides with laughter, because they think the name Tecelinga is comical, and then they are suddenly threatened with prison if they ever use the name Tötschling again. Valli: Gentlemen, Tötschling, Tecelinga, those are indeed important subjects, if you consider it closely, but in the meantime have we not all learned that . . . Meraner: No. I have learned nothing. And, by the way, I don't want to learn anything. I have a right not to have to learn anything! Before God, I have a right to do that. Neri sat for a while with his arms folded and did not say another word. He listened to Meraner's homily, and when Meraner was finished he still sat there silent for a while, still with his arms folded, and then said: In spite of everything, I still say that your Gasser wrote that. He and no one else. Valli: But Giuseppe, why do you say *our Gasser*? That's not fair, it's open to question. If Gasser did write it, then we want nothing more to do with him. Gruber: Where does Neri get the idea that Gasser wrote it? Gasser isn't here at the moment. Valli: Well, a few people think, I would even have to say that it is almost the unanimous opinion, that probably . . . Gasser . . . well, that Gasser is the author. What is, actually, the problem with the paper? What you read there is simply and solely a description. Valli: Well, yes, but the paper does make an unambiguous political point. Gruber: What point? Valli: Please do not misunderstand. He, himself, is not prejudiced against Gasser, and whether Gasser actually took part in the attack upon Herr Alois Zurner is certainly not proven. (Growls: What is meant by taking part? Say what you like, he planned it! He probably arranged the whole thing himself.) Valli: There is absolutely no proof of that, and he, Valli, did not think it probable, because Josef is a sensible lad, he doesn't do things like that, and as for writing anonymous letters, he doesn't do that either. Neri: He does something quite different. Kerschbaumer meanwhile had also entered the bar and was listening to the conversation with great interest, as the name Gasser was mentioned frequently. Because he was so interested in Katharine Gasser, the actress, he was also interested in anything that affected her brother Josef and indeed the whole family. He was also of the opinion that the Italian university assistant could be behind the pamphlet that was posted up behind Nussbaumer's and in other places. And why him in particular, asked Neri. Kerschbaumer shrugged his shoulders. It had merely occurred to him, he said. Neri waved this aside. Kerschbaumer: Ever since he's been here, strange things have been happening. First, Maretsch and Moreth had been beaten up, then Zurner, then there's this flyer, and now I've seen this Italian here for the first time. Everyone is talking about him. Kerschbaumer looked around innocently, he had said everything so casually, so simply, just off the cuff. Huber: The Italian talks and talks, I've noticed that too. He doesn't leave you in peace. He'll nail you down on something you've said, and suddenly you find yourself having said something that you didn't want to say at all. Young Moreth: He'll also impute some reason or other to you for doing this or that. Huber: Exactly! He twists everything you say. And all the time he goes on talking about everything under the sun, really repulsive and completely unmanly. Young Moreth: I've heard that he's an Apocalypticist. Huber: A what? All the people in Nussbaumer's looked at Moreth inquiringly. Moreth: An Apocalypticist. Someone who believes in the impending end of the world or, at least, who constantly preaches it. The end of the world, you understand! Valli: But he had never heard this Zanetti preach about the end of the world. Moreth: And if these apocalypticists aren't on about the end of the world then at least they're talking about a general conspiracy or something of the sort. Valli: Can you explain it to us more precisely? Huber: But please don't make it so complicated. Meraner: Exactly. Not so complicated. We all want to understand some of it, so don't make it so complicated. Neri: Today's youth always talks complicatedly, they do it because they don't want to be understood, and in fact there's no way they can be understood, and they know that, that's why they talk like that. Valli: Now, hold your horses. We're not talking here about Moreth, but about this Florentine. Neri: Why *this* Florentine? Why do you say *Moreth*, but *this Florentine*? Then instead of Moreth say *this Klausener*! But there was one thing that he had to agree about: this Zanetti appeared highly suspicious to him. And why is he suddenly giving a lecture? It's all very peculiar. Huber: What sort of a lecture? Everyone looked at Huber as though he were the only person who didn't know what everyone else was talking about. Valli: The university assistant, Zanetti, was giving a lecture that evening at eight o'clock, in the town hall, didn't you know? Huber: No. Neri: But there are placards all over the place. Huber: What, you mean something else has been posted? Do people here spend all their time posting things up nowadays? Besides, he didn't read the placards in any case. Meraner: you don't read a newspaper either. Huber: What do you mean by that? Meraner: I don't mean anything at all by that. I was just saying that you do not read the newspaper. Huber stood up and shook his fist threateningly. I can read that, d'you understand, my fist! All you mean is that because you are all so profound, then I'm an imbecile, but that's where you're mistaken. I didn't know anything about a lecture, and now I do, and now be quiet, said Huber, looking around menacingly. What's the lecture about anyway? Would I be interested in it? Meraner: The title of the lecture is *The Modern Economic Zone, South Tyrol*. Moreth said that he thought the title was *Ethics in the Modern Economic Zone*. Meraner: He was sure that South Tyrol was mentioned in the title. Why should Zanetti give a lecture in Klausen, of all places, if South Tyrol was not even mentioned in the title? No one would go to it. Valli: The lecture, just a moment, he had the invitation here, the title as originally announced was: *The Modern Economic Zone in the Light of Philosophical Ethics, with Particular Reference to the Autonomous Provinces*. Aha, someone said, so it is South Tyrol after all. When he says "the autonomous provinces" he means South Tyrol. But why as originally announced, what was that supposed to mean? Has the title been changed? Valli: Actually, Zanetti said yesterday that he would lecture on a different subject, but the placards had already been posted, but it doesn't matter what he's going to talk about, that was a matter for the Education Association, the title of the new lecture . . . one moment, he'd made a note of it, he wasn't quite . . . Ah, here (reading from a slip of paper): the title is *Ontology and Consciousness, Hypotheses on* . . . (stumbling, reading again): . . . *Hypotheses on Heidegger.*

On whom? someone shouted. Valli: On Heidegger. Huber: Which Heidegger then? Valli: No idea, he didn't know either. In any case people immediately forgot the incomprehensible title, and above all they forgot the word ontology at once, it didn't register with anyone; apparently it was a word to which, as soon as it was uttered, one turned a deaf ear. Valli now asked Moreth finally to explain what he was going to say about Zanetti with regard to conspiracy and the end of the world. Everybody renewed the siege of young Moreth, again begging him to say it as simply and comprehensibly as possible. Moreth said that wherever Zanetti appeared he presented certain apocalyptic theories both about the world economy or its total collapse, as well as the ecological burden upon the world and the dialectically necessary emergence of certain ecological and even terrorist movements. These would surface just as inevitably as *the brown of the leaves in autumn*; he'd heard that from Zanetti's own mouth. Huber: As the brown of the leaves in autumn, aha. By the way, what was it he had just said about terrorism? Had that got something to do with Klausen? If there are terrorists here, then we'll arm ourselves and take things into our own hands. As sure as my name's Huber. At this point, the conversation became more and more chaotic. Someone suggested that old Perluttner might be behind the placarding. This idea was hotly debated for all of three minutes. The man, people said, was notorious for attacking all sorts of things. Perluttner had once demonstrated, on the square in front of the church, with a cardboard sign attached to his walking stick, in support of . . . no one could remember what had occasioned the demonstration. In any case, at the time, the whole town had known that old Perluttner was standing there. For several hours he had remained in front of the church portal with his placard, as if rooted there, and then, for a further hour, he had walked round and round shouting a variety of slogans, until eventually some people had gotten rid of him. Now and again, different groups of Klauseners had kept on turning up in front of the church, just to have a look at Perluttner as he was demonstrating. Why shouldn't Perluttner suddenly take it into his head to grumble about the dam, the road construction, and all the traffic? After all it was quite conceivable. But the idea was immediately dropped again, for on the one hand no one thought Perluttner capable of writing such a detailed text, with such precise descriptions, and on the other it was quite impossible for Perluttner to have put the text on the internet—the old man had no knowledge of such things. Besides which the person in question had trespassed to reach the side of the tourist association. They talked about the placard in question for quite a time at Nussbaumer's; still other customers who had all read the text outside came in, and more and more of them appeared insulted and irritated by it. Why does young Gasser insult and abuse Klausen in such a repellent and despicable manner? someone shouted. We don't want our town to be insulted. We want to be proud of our town. Anyone who insults our town insults us. And anyone who insults us should clear out. Of course, that was a statement that was just as completely logical as it was completely meaningless! someone shouted into the room with rhetorical emphasis. People even clapped; others, however, laughed. Wine was ordered. Gruber left Nussbaumer's again straightaway, in order to go to the Gassers. On his way out of the restaurant it occurred to him that not far from the placard, that had simply been left hanging there as though it were a municipal announcement that everyone should read, there was also a placard

with Dürer's well-known engraving on it, a placard that was advertising something that did have to do with Klausen. The engraving
was used for all sorts of things, because the Klausen drawn by Dürer
is completely idyllic and admirably suited for publicity. Dürer's *Great
Good Fortune* is Klausen's great good fortune. What a lot of people
Dürer's name draws to Klausen! Gruber was looking thoughtfully at
the placard, but then he simply tore it down and threw it into the
nearest wastebasket. Yes, an aggressive mood prevailed everywhere.
Towards noon a whole group of people were assembled in Josef Gasser's parents' apartment. Never before had so many people gathered
in the small apartment. A great deal, both detailed and sketchy, was
said about this later on. Paolucci stood by the bay window almost the
whole time, stroking his beard, now and again making notes, and
drinking a great deal of coffee. Sonja Maretsch was sitting on the
couch most of the time gazing straight ahead quietly, but she did get
up once and phoned the Piedmontese woman at Castle Branzoll for
some reason or another. Christian Marestch was also there and was
talking about the measurements they had made. He had a small band-
age on his head. Paolucci kept asking him questions. In the middle of
their conversation, they began to quarrel about something, but the
others couldn't make out what they were quarreling about because,
in spite of their agitation, the two of them were talking as softly as
possible. Kati was only there for a short while, and she just sat there
the whole time with her elbows on top of the table behind which she
was sitting, holding her clenched fists in front of her mouth. She held
this pose for almost a quarter of an hour and seemed to be thinking,
in great haste, about a host of different things; then she left the group
and went back to her hotel, perhaps because Paolucci was there and

kept looking over at her, and Kati was not feeling in the mood to be looked at. When she took her leave, Paolucci lost his self-control for a moment and looked at her in astonishment, but did not dare to say a word and quickly turned away again to stare out of the bay window onto the street. Others were there too, Frau Finozzi and Zanetti, who, strangely enough, didn't say a word the whole time, not even about the lecture that people were looking forward to that evening; he did not even like people to talk to him about it. For some reason or another alderman Valli, who had in the meantime developed a great liking for Josef Gasser, joined the group. Even Perluttner turned up and sat down on the bench near the door with his stick in his hand. Frau Gasser was sitting in the aforementioned chair. She was sitting on this chair the whole time and seemed, at that moment, to be in a state of shock or, at least, very reflective. She scarcely greeted people as they came in, and everyone noticed it. She just let everything wash over her. She looked once at Paolucci, who was still standing at the bay window. As though absently, she said, Josef had also stood in the bay window like that, at their last meeting. He had been nervous, silent. That was the foundation stone of all evil, she said. No one understood what she meant by *the foundation stone of all evil*, but people preferred not to ask because she said it all in such a strange tone of voice. Some of them wanted to leave again, but Frau Gasser suddenly jumped up, went hurriedly to the people in question, and drew them back into their seats. This had an inhibiting effect upon everyone. She then sat down on her chair again. Gasser's mother now proceeded to repeat, almost word for word, all the thoughts that Gasser had had about the chair and confirmed these thoughts to everyone, but she gave them a startling psychological twist. She suddenly maintained that the rise of her daughter had *quite naturally* had the effect of making her increasingly neglect and even consciously belittle herself. That was why she had fetched the chair from the attic. Only then had Kati's triumph been made complete (by the chair). Kati's advancement grew more lofty the more deeply she, her mother, debased herself—namely, to the place where she really belonged. Her brother, Josef, she said, had seen all this but he had not wished to participate in the process (alas). His sister's advancement had spoiled him, she said. She, the mother, had not been spoiled by her advancement; she had fetched the chair from the attic. Now she was what she had always been, and Kati, by her advancement, had made clear to all the Klauseners what all of them had always been: nothing. Laughing: For that reason she, Frau Gasser, had married her husband, that's why she had had children, that's why she was living here in this small apartment, for the same reason that's why anything that happened did happen and for the sake of completeness she had remembered this chair, brought it down from the attic, and sat down on it. As time passed, she had even developed a liking for sitting on the chair; as soon as she woke up she thought of the chair and of sitting on the chair and watching the streets through the bay window, like her son, like Gasser . . . *et cetera*. That was her greatest desire and only joy. The woman was looking very strange as she said this, so that you might think that she had lost control of herself and was going from one extreme to the other, for suddenly she would be praising her son to the skies and talking of his total innocence only to be condemning him all the more harshly the next minute. As she did this she clutched the aforementioned chair. It was all extremely pathetic and irritating . . . Obviously she had been deeply disturbed by what had happened and the accusations that had been leveled at her son, and possibly she was only humiliating herself to such an extent in front everybody because she believed that her son was doing exactly the same thing and his humiliation had made her despair. That was of course complete nonsense. Sonja told Frau Gasser that her remarks about the chair and her worthlessness and Kati would only lead to people's implying that exactly the same reasons underlay Gasser's actions (which led her to ask herself what she meant exactly by *actions*, since for a long time no one had known anything about Gasser's actions, everyone had simply supposed this and that). But Frau Gasser did not understand what Sonja was getting at, because conditions in the world, as far as she was concerned, were obviously determined once and for all, and, for her, there was a totally compelling logic to a Josef Gasser's being condemned to carry his own nullity around with him—like a rucksack—wherever he went, his whole life long, to the point of desperation. (She: And now he does despair.) Frau Gasser's psychological remarks gave many a person in the room seriously to think. How could the woman say such crazy things? Where on earth did she get all this nonsense from? Confined for years to her apartment, visited only two or three times a week by a Frau Huber or a Frau Unterleitner, surrounded the whole time by her magazines and the afternoon TV shows, she had obviously developed a, so to speak, popular-psychological picture of her own situation that had, in addition, contained some really diabolical traits. However, Frau Gasser's diatribe only lasted a few minutes, and when it was over she suddenly seemed quite normal again and entertained everyone in a very friendly manner with strudel and coffee. Admittedly since that time Frau Gasser's theory—Gasser is obviously in

despair out of envy, because of his own inconspicuous role—has persisted. This could be the best explanation of all his (alleged) actions,
because psychological patterns of this sort are such that they can be
used to explain *anything*. It is possible to explain a human being by
this means, that is, by psychology, whenever you want to (it is amaz-
ingly simple and thus so beguiling), and the speaker does not even
notice that he is always talking exclusively about himself and his own
theories, which he then imposes on the world and the whole human
race, and not talking about the object that he is observing (the person, for example, Gasser). The man in the street subsequently knew
one thing only: the psychological model of explanation. This it what
reduced Gasser to such a handy tidbit that he could easily be mauled
in the arena. In this way he was, so to speak, finally made palatable.
Everyone now had hold of Gasser, because everyone now *knew* something about him. The details of the event, the clues, all that was in
dispute were, first and foremost, a matter for the police and for foren-
sics, that is, not available to be expressed publicly (unless in the form
of a rumor), but the psychological pattern that had been discovered,
or, alternatively, its application to Gasser, was concrete *knowledge* and
was freely available to, and could be used by, everyone. Incidentally,
a few people soon left the Gassers' apartment; only Gruber, Sonja,
Paolucci, and alderman Valli stayed behind. There was a strange
mood in the room. Everything was subdued, muffled; the awful fur-
nishings added to the mood—the dark wood paneling gave the impression that the roof might soon collapse with terrific force upon the
guests. Finally, alderman Valli, who had hardly said a word the whole
time, took his farewell. He stopped once more in the doorway, however, and suddenly asked a few questions. He asked certain things

about Delazer, no one quite understood why, and Paolucci gave him some very speculative answers, conjecture upon conjecture (he seemed to suggest that everyone there was free to invent whatever he or she liked). Valli was really amazed at everything. Everybody was talking about this Laner and this Delazer, he said, everyone was behaving as though something immeasurably bad had happened, but he (Valli) could not understand what it was that had happened; for one thing, it had in the meantime been almost certainly demonstrated that neither Auer, nor that loafer Badowsky, nor even Zanetti (". . . Zanetti, what an absurd suspicion! Whose idea was that? . . .") had taken part in the attack upon Zurner. Gasser most probably had had nothing to do with it either. But, on the other hand, at least *something must have happened* or else there would be no occasion to talk about these things. So Valli inquired with interest but received no clear information and declared that obviously no one could find out what had actually happened. Certainly Zurner had been set upon. But that seemed to belong to the past; new developments had come to light and new consequences were to be expected from these new developments, worse consequences than the mere ill-treatment of a simple citizen of Brixen. What could not be foreseen frightened people like Valli and kept them stretched upon a brutal rack. Then Valli, standing in the doorframe, took a paper from his pocket and asked what the title of the day's lecture was supposed to mean. As he said this, he looked Sonja, Gruber, and Paolucci searchingly in the face, as though he already mistrusted them before they had given any sort of answer. Valli: He had looked up Heidegger in the encyclopedia, he seems to have been a philosopher, that much he could make out, but . . . was he dangerous? Paolucci: Why dangerous? Valli: It is not known. None of us

knows what Zanetti will be talking about. Do you know that there is
a theory that Zanetti was the author of the pamphlet, with the intent
of upsetting people, with the sole purpose of getting crowds of them
to come to his lecture that evening—which they thought would con-
tain something important. Yes, they are certainly expecting something important . . . And no one knows what he will be talking about
or even exactly why he is going to be talking on this subject. Sonja:
What gives people the idea that he could say anything important in
his lecture? He's giving a lecture about a philosopher, that's nothing
unusual in an adult education class. Now, said Valli, you're saying
that because of the theory I just mentioned, the theory about the pamphlet. Otherwise the pamphlet would be quite superfluous . . . Sonja:
But that's arguing in circles. One thing is proved by another, and
then the other thing is proved by the first, that's complete nonsense.
Valli: Yes, nonsense . . . he didn't know . . . he himself didn't know.
And then the word *ontology*. He had also looked that word up in the
dictionary, but he couldn't fully understand what it said about the
word there. What he meant to say was that he couldn't imagine that
anyone could, or would even *want* to, give a lecture about it, it seemed
so obscure and out of context, you could think it was just about mere
. . . mere illusion. By the way, it was said that Zanetti believed in the
apocalypse. Aha, said Paolucci. Valli looked him meaningfully in the
face. Then he left. Turning around: And did they know that Gasser
had recently claimed to be an architect? Paolucci said it was no use
asking him; he had recently been spending all his time in Milan and
for weeks now had hardly been in Klausen. So, said Valli, for weeks,
and looked at him in astonishment. I didn't know that for weeks . . .
He was looking back and forth between Gruber and Paolucci again,

his face filled with great mistrust. Perhaps, in the meantime, Valli had come to mistrust everyone. He: Incidentally, he had not, he thought, pretended to be an architect but rather an engineer. It's very strange for him to pretend to be an engineer. That's certainly significant, certainly that is significant, he said, and after that he disappeared. Then he came back once more and even went back into the front room, where Frau Gasser was still sitting. Valli said that there had been some talk about an overcoat, an overcoat of Gasser's, he had learned of it by chance and now people were speculating this and that, just because of the coat. Did Frau Gasser know anything about the coat? She: I know nothing at all about my son's coat. Does he have a coat? What I am supposed to know about a coat? Josef had been abroad for many years, comes back, doesn't come to visit, only comes to visit now and again and now people are asking me about a coat. A coat! Valli: There is indeed a coat, it was found in the Cellar, they say it was hanging there, at first no one noticed it but at some point it was noticed, and now it's being said that it could be Gasser's coat. It's been taken to the police now, or perhaps just to the town hall. Besides, it's quite unimportant, it just happened to occur to him, meanwhile, you start noticing the most remarkable things. Yes, said Paolucci, apparently everything now becomes a sign of something. As he said this, Valli once more wrinkled his brow and looked at him pensively, for perhaps half a minute, and then walked out of the apartment. He left the others somewhat mystified. Frau Gasser was suddenly very upset because of the coat and said she had to go to the authorities about it at once. She made several references to the *abandoned coat*, and Sonja said she could go with her, she knew Gasser's coat, the landlord of the Cellar knew the coat as well, and in view of that, she thought it unlikely that the landlord would have taken it to the police, he would probably more likely have left it where it was, *et cetera*. Then, while they were talking about this possibly completely unimportant coat and had become caught up in a strange bout of activity (Frau Gasser for her part was already standing, with her coat on, ready to leave), the telephone rang. They all looked at one another. Then they all looked at the telephone, which stood on a chest. For a time no one thought of answering it. Everyone was obviously confused. Finally Sonja answered it. She listened to someone for a few seconds, said something, and handed the receiver to Paolucci. He picked up the conversation, sat down on the bench with the telephone in his hand, and suddenly jumped up again and looked thoughtfully up at the ceiling. He seemed to be focusing intently on one spot up there, so precisely and so intently that all the others also looked up at the same spot although there was nothing there. Paolucci stayed like that for a minute or two. Then he went to the bay window and looked out of it, still with the receiver to his ear. Yes, all right, he said finally, and bring a photographer with you! This has to be recorded, everything must be recorded in pictures. The public has to know of this, of what's happening out there. Then he hung up. The others looked at him expectantly. Paolucci looked very confused, but suddenly he smiled. All right, everybody, he said, Ploder castle is being stormed! . . . everybody looked at the Gasser's wall clock. It was half past eleven in the morning . . . This event, the so-called storming of Ploder castle, needs to be looked into more closely. The police operation at the castle did explain some things, but, as a whole, what the Klauseners learned bit by bit as the day went on only made everything more confused and incomprehensible, and absolutely unbelievable theories emerged. The description of what happened has to be anticipated here in order to make the extent of the happening comprehensible. In the afternoon—still hours before Zanetti's lecture—the news that the police and carabinieri had joined forces and stormed Ploder castle had meanwhile spread over the whole district. At first the news seemed to be almost logical, and it even seemed inevitable to many that they had actually been waiting for it the whole time, without being really conscious of it (this is a remarkable human characteristic—namely, that after the fact people believe that they already had a presentiment of exactly what was to happen later on). In any case, of course, some of those who spoke particularly emphatically about what happened were, as always, already drunk at this hour. The strange thing about this sort of news, that spreads like wildfire, is of course that the text can never be confirmed. That is why it always grows more and more wonderful as it travels from mouth to mouth, until it finally resembles a spectacular firework display. There were tales of police buses, of whole packs of dogs, of large numbers of arrests that were said to have been made: all this is supposed to have taken place by the light of innumerable searchlights. (Though, in any case, the so-called storming took place in the morning and it was all over by the time they had looked at the clock in Gasser's sitting room at half past eleven. Searchlights, of course, had not been used.) Dozens of policemen, all heavily armed and wearing bullet-proof vests, were said to have taken part . . . However, it was not clear why the castle had been stormed. If the castle really had been stormed, someone must have barricaded himself in there. Had the Moroccan and Albanian families dug themselves in there? (But why?) Had someone else dug himself in? No one knew anything about that. Some thought it was scandalous to storm the castle. They even seemed absolutely certain of it; they were morally outraged. But when they were asked to say more specifically what the scandal was, they were unable to answer. They said that the poor Moroccan and Albanian families were now standing out on the street; many, they said, had certainly been arrested. This view seemed later to have been reinforced. There seemed to have been a logical reason for storming the castle, but if anyone had asked wherein this logic lay they would surely have received very vague answers. Some said it cannot go on like this, things have got to be cleaned out up there. Others (Perluttner for example) said that, from the Italian side, the whole police system in South Tyrol was state terrorism. (As can be seen from this statement, Perluttner hated the Italian authorities even more than the migrants.) Yet others maintained that only Gasser and his cronies knew the answer to all the questions and accordingly should, in the long run, be held accountable for anything that happened now. The latter view was held by a group that had, in the meanwhile, formed around Giuseppe Neri. And just as the clouds gradually start to break up and the sky grows clear again after a storm, so the excitement about the storming of Ploder castle abated and things were seen in a less and less spectacular light. But now as to the event itself. Paolucci and the others went straight from Frau Gasser's to Brixen to observe things on the spot. They found a demonstration taking place. A small crowd of people had congregated in front of the castle and, as time passed, more and more people of all sorts and conditions joined them; they had brought hastily produced banners and cardboard signs with them and were making a tremendous noise with percussion instruments—some of them improvised. They called upon the residents of the castle to come out and demonstrate with them. No one heeded the invitation; instead the castle's residents looked timidly at the crowd and were at least as afraid of them as they were of the police and all the others. Discussions were taking place even with the carabinieri who were present because of the rally. Still more people came and joined them. Someone gave a captivating speech about the social impoverishment of those seeking asylum in Europe, and Italy's historical responsibility, Italy's responsibility towards its own history, for not only had Germany had its Hitler, but Italy had had its Mussolini, so they too had a duty. We want to help you, we are with you, shouted the demonstrators up to the windows. These were immediately closed. A number of prominent persons arrived in front of Ploder castle, even the acting mayor of Brixen appeared and tried to calm things down, for the mood towards the police, and especially state power, was growing increasingly heated. The police operation was interpreted as an obviously arbitrary measure and as mere harassment on the part of the authorities. However, the extent of the police operation now appeared in a more realistic light. It could not really be called a storming. True, a sort of raid had taken place, but the police contingent was not nearly as large as it was first alleged to have been, and no significant resistance or even digging in had taken place. A few of the castle's residents had, surprisingly, actually been taken to the police station; there were violent arguments about the reason for this. Foreigners have no rights in this country, they are outlawed, it was said, the state was showing its true face, it was said. The successive destruction of the whole environment in the Eisack valley was only tolerated for the sake of money, yet suddenly the authorities were acting aggressively towards a handful of foreigners. This was a rationalization, a rationalization, cried Badowsky, who had suddenly reappeared as if from nowhere. He was called on to explain what he meant by the word *rationalization*, but he could not; perhaps he had just heard it somewhere. Badowsky soon became one of the main speakers at the event. He stood up on a haystack and made a speech against globalization, against imperialism and fascism, but in the process kept looking out of the corner of his eye at the police, to see whether perhaps they might get it into their heads to arrest him because of the assault in the Brixen palace garden. People, demonstrators, Brixeners! he shouted, what we have seen done here today, in the name of our state, is a disgrace. They have the money, they have the power, we . . . we have no money, and by the way, we also have no power, but that doesn't seem to be enough for them, they also wish to provoke us, for in proceeding against our Moroccan and our Albanian fellow-citizens in this fascist manner, they provoke us. If they slap them in the face and arrest them, they are slapping us in the face, they should be arresting us, we shall not stop resisting, for when we rise up and take action together against this barbarism then we shall be setting an example, and this gathering, Brixeners, people, and I can see a number of Germans here among us, this gathering is a signal. There was a good deal of applause, but most people did not understand what Badowsky was talking about. Nor did they understand why Badowsky spoke of *our state* when he was certainly not an Italian or even a South Tyrolean, but a German and, more precisely, a Westphalian. After this came an attack on globalization. The attack was, actually, completely unmotivated in the context of the demonstration, but nonetheless some people listened. Badowsky called for the craziest things. He called for a boycott of goods, demanded immediate payments and a total forgiveness of Third World debts, then he demanded an immediate ban on the building of roads and airports in Europe, and finally he actually demanded customs duties. There! he shouted, and pointed with his outstretched arm to the autobahn on the other side of the valley, there is the dragon that is laying waste to your valley and bringing money to the powerful, kill this dragon, destroy the trade, smash each and every thing they tell you to, *et cetera*. These were, as many people thought, very crazy things that he was saying. Furthermore, he kept on laughing absolutely hysterically while saying these things, and it seemed as though he had learned it all by heart and was repeating it like a parrot. But it was also obvious that he was seized with enthusiasm—he believed that it was a great moment for him. As he stood on his haystack, he was more and more carried away by his demands for the destruction of this and that. He now demanded, among other things, that the mayor of Brixen and the town's police chief be hounded out of office, and, as a movement ran through the police who were present and they began to make motions to remove the speaker—who was growing ever crazier and crazier—from his perch, Badowsky suddenly managed to get down from the haystack and, somehow or other, disappear. Auer was standing among the crowd, drunk, and was clapping and applauding enthusiastically, for he had never experienced anything as strange as this mass of people, and what made him most elated was the complete absence of any reason for all that was happening. The demonstration lasted for several hours; it was almost as though the castle were being besieged. Paolucci chatted for a while with Auer and now finally discovered—because he absolutely had to know—what was in the mysterious letter that Gasser had given Auer in the Cellar just before he disappeared. That was the letter that Auer had said nothing about at the time, he had just put it aside in disgust and Badowsky had read it that evening but had obviously not understood it, because he had been far too drunk. At the time, everyone had wondered what the contents of letter were; and ever since Gasser had taken center stage, Paolucci had wondered even more. He had imagined God knows what important matter was treated in the letter and had expected it to be something completely political. However the contents of the letter were only as follows: A German Ministry (Province of Brandenburg, Headquarters, Potsdam) was informing Auer that he was to receive a grant for some reason or another. Auer still had the letter in his pants' pocket (he had forgotten it was there) and showed it to Paolucci. The letter was completely crumpled up. It had even landed in the dirt during the demonstration and stayed there, for the simple reason that Auer wanted nothing to do with the grant and certainly not with a ministry, the whole thing seemed vulgar and suspicious to him. Paolucci, however, was completely at a loss as to why anyone should refuse money that he was apparently to receive for doing nothing but what he did the whole time anyway—writing and drawing. He asked him what it all meant. If he, Auer, wanted to lead an existence as an artist then, he said, the grant would be of the greatest importance for him. Auer refused to discuss the matter and looked downright disgusted by the phrase *existence as an artist* (for one thing he abhorred the word existence, he had no idea what it was supposed to mean, and, in contrast to Pareith, he would never have thought of himself as an artist; he would rather be described by words like *fool*, or *idiot*,

or *deceiver* but not by the word artist, that was too sacred for him. He
was also not in a position to organize a cult around himself, apart
from what he produced, all he was in position to do was to drink all
the time—that was his only interest. It is true that today—after his
death—there is a cult and literary tourists sit around in the Cellar
and exchange details, *et cetera*, about Auer). Auer: He had not applied
for the money from Potsdam and he would not accept it, he had not
needed the money for a long time and he didn't need it now. But of
course you need money, said Paolucci, you haven't got a penny, you
cannot go on living as you do now. Auer said he didn't need money.
He didn't want any money. He didn't want to have anything to do
with such things. And he was not about to give him any further explanation. Then he said in a rather mysterious way: Gasser would
understand, he could explain it to him, he, Auer, could not explain
it, of course, Gasser would also not explain anything, beyond a certain point you no longer talk any more, you are, on the contrary,
past it, and once this particular point has been reached, people like
Badowsky suddenly begin to attach themselves to you and start talking themselves, their talk grows more and more independent, and
finally certain things take place because this independence has been
achieved, but by then you yourself have long since had nothing more
to do with it. Paolucci looked at him in astonishment. What did he
mean by that? he asked, while yet another chorus, demanding free-
dom and unconditional rights for asylum seekers and migrants, arose.
Auer made no reply but stamped hard upon the letter from the German ministry that lay in a muddy puddle on the ground. Auer even
glared at it angrily, which was a great surprise to Paolucci, for he had
never seen Auer lose his temper. But it only lasted a moment, for then

Auer ceased to take any notice of Paolucci, he had completely forgotten him from one moment to the next, just as he had the letter on the
ground . . . in the midst of the confusion, as some people later maintained, Gasser had suddenly appeared. No one could confirm this,
but the rumor that Gasser had been present, that he had stayed on the
fringe of the demonstration for a while, watching everything from a
certain distance, obstinately persisted, and it was even said that he
spoke to one or another of the people, just as though he were giving
certain directions. In any case, it later transpired that this Gasser,
who is supposed to have appeared there, was merely a phantom, a
manifestation transmuted from the evening to the middle of the day.
People also believe in appearances of the Virgin Mary. When someone maintains that they have seen the Virgin Mary, people will immediately appear who believe that person unconditionally, and they,
for their part, will begin to quarrel bitterly with those who deny the
visions of the Virgin; that's well known. In the same way, they saw
Josef Gasser in front of the castle. The vision is the highest form of
rumor, and he who has such visions is, of course, always irrefutable
(he can either be believed or not). They even maintained that Gasser
had definitely contributed to the fact that the demonstration had broken up and that people had finally gone home, and even if they had
not seen it with their own eyes they had at least been told of it. After
the end of the demonstration in front of the castle, one group went up
in the direction of Elvas to the Guggerhof to partake of something
strong. Gruber was among them, Paolucci and Auer too, who drank
perhaps five or six Nusseler,[4] fairly green Nusseler, in a short period

4. A liqueur made in South Tyrol from unripe walnuts, schnapps and sugar (the
more unripe ("green") the nuts, the more potent the drink.

of time and, of course, ate nothing. About 7:00 P.M., more and more people were to be found in the community center. A word about the Klausen community center, so that some idea may gained of how an event held by the adult education association may be portrayed. It's a formerly modern hall dating from the early nineteen-eighties, with a restaurant adjoining it, built in an architectural style that actually belongs to the seventies. It has no windows, there are partitions that can be pushed aside, and there is a bare wood and metal stage at the front; the seating consists of single chairs, with green upholstered seats, that can be hooked together. Otherwise the room is quite bare. Its senseless functionalism (the partitions for instance have never been used for anything and the extendible stage has, of course, never been extended) comes from a time when everything architectural had to be functional, even if the functions were never used and were there simply because someone wanted them. Actually, all the communities who built community halls of this sort are today absolutely dumbfounded by them, and the only reason they do not raze them is so that they will not be a total embarrassment. They even praise the halls to this very day . . . (on Pareith's *A View of the Town of Klausen* the community center was not to be seen, a meadow could be seen in its place). That is the sort of hall that the Klausen community center is. A few people were already sitting on their green upholstered seats, others were drinking beer, wine, or schnapps in the restaurant, and others again were helping themselves to the drinks buffet in the anteroom. Quite a few were standing in front of the several placards that had been hung up by the adult education association advertising its activities and were reading the title of the day's lecture:

*The Modern Economic Space in the Light of Philosophical Ethics,
with Special Reference to the Autonomous Provinces.*

The title seemed a weighty one to them, splendid and, above all, learned; it raised certain expectations, but many would have been just as incapable of expressing in words the expectations that it aroused in them as they would have been formulating the questions that arose from it, because for most people the title remained totally obscure. People could, it is true, imagine something of what Modern Economic Space meant—the word space (economic *space*) sounded modern, like something quite definite; people knew that (for recently everyone was using the word *space* for all sorts of different things), but people felt somewhat insecure when they thought more deeply about it. Philosophical ethics: the expression was very unclear to the great majority of people. Only a few of the audience could envisage anything distinct in the word philosophy; the word ethics, on the other hand, had become fashionable lately—that is not to say, however, that most people understood it any better because of that. As to the formulation *autonomous provinces*, some did not know that there were any other autonomous provinces besides their own. There were also a few Klauseners who had no clear idea of what the word *autonomous* was actually supposed to mean, although they had been using the term constantly for almost thirty years. Here and there, voices were to be heard, saying that Zanetti had changed his subject and was not going to speak about the modern economic space. What a shame, said some. Nonsense, said others. Zanetti, they said, was a friend of Gasser, the leader of the gang who had disappeared, and his subject was the economy, Italian economy, so Zanetti would also discuss this subject, nothing else made any sense and was, strictly speaking, unthinkable. Sonja and Paolucci were standing in the vestibule with some others and were talking animatedly about what had happened that afternoon in the castle in Brixen. It had been announced in the meanwhile that the police had found some things there, and rumors about what these things were had intensified. Various people walked past in the vestibule, recognized the journalist, joined in the conversation, listened for a while, and then took part—while heatedly expressing their views—for a short time in the debate, only to leave again and look for a seat in the hall. There was a mood of excitement among these people, although they all looked as though they were taking part in a ceremony, for they were already holding various aperitifs in their hands and seemed to be full of anticipation. (There were also some Germans in the vestibule, all tourists in small groups, apparently seeking an evening's entertainment; many of them appeared intimidated by the drinks displayed on the buffet table, others appeared more daring.) People in the crowd around Paolucci were saying in general that the storming of the castle had been fully justified, as the state of affairs had later shown. Rumor had it that narcotics had been found—marijuana, cocaine, and heroin. Aha, some people said and raised their eyebrows. Others said, you came across that everywhere these days, it had been expected. Someone: Where there are people like that, then you always find something. A neighbor: The Yugoslavs trade *mainly* in heroin, everyone knows that. Someone: And in spite of that they let them come in. Another man: That's because Rome is a hydra, *et cetera*. Paolucci said there wasn't a single Yugoslav in the castle, there were Albanians there. Response: What difference does that make? Someone shouted: Those people from back there, they're all the same! Paolucci: And we up front here, we are also all the same. If they call you an Italian and not a South Tyrolean, you get red in the face and now you don't even want to distinguish an Albanian from a Yugoslav. The man being spoken to: Why was he comparing him with those people there? He didn't understand. What was he getting at? Another man: He wasn't implying anything. And you shut up! We're in public here. Public, said the other, aren't we allowed to say what we think in public any more? In today's *Press Review* the editor said that the people in the Eisack valley were, naturally, upset that the province was buying up the houses along the railroad and intended to place the non-EU citizens in them, do you understand, *naturally* they are upset. And he would say so openly on TV, *naturally* upset. And I am upset. I'm upset about it (even if they are keeping it a secret) and that is only *natural*, so there you are! The other man: I saw the *Press Review* too. The editor used the word in exactly the opposite sense. What he wanted to say was: The province is buying the houses along the railroad in order to place these people in them, and the people in the Eisack valley are getting upset again, just as they get upset about anything foreign (to the extent that it doesn't bring any money in) especially now that it has come out that they are non-EU-citizens. That was a criticism of us. A few Germans were listening to the conversation with interest and broke in on the discussion. A: Non-EU-citizen, what a word, that's just sweet talk. B (quietly, upset, aside): Riffraff and vermin that's what it means. C: I've got absolutely nothing against them, but they should stay at home. D: We don't go over there. E: Certainly, they are different cultures, and you can accept that, why shouldn't there be other cultures, but they are after all alien to us. F: How you do go on. I am happy and content with or without foreigners. G: We prosper, and always have, at the expense of others, and now they are coming to us, we brought it upon ourselves. H: We are the light . . . I: And they are the moths. K: We've certainly deserved it. Yes, we've lived in luxury here in Europe while billions of other people have scarcely enough to eat. C: But we aren't the universal welfare factory. D: We built our prosperity with our own hands, and those of our ancestors. E: What prosperity? The economic data grows worse all the time . . . A Klausener to Paolucci: And the three Pakistanis? What about the three Pakistanis? Paolucci: What about them? The Klausener: Haven't they been arrested too? Paolucci: Why should they have been arrested? The other man: Why shouldn't they have been? After all some stolen goods had been found, or so he'd been told. Paolucci: They say that three TV sets, that are thought to have been stolen, have been found, as well as other stolen goods like watches or chains with some cheap charms attached. (To the general public): Some weapons were certainly found in a shed, not far from the place where that group of demonstrators, or agitators, who were passing through a few days ago, had been drinking and spending the night and had roasted an ox. That is to say, weapons were not actually found, but boxes of ammunition were, empty ammunition boxes according to a report in the newspapers. According to other people, one or two hand grenades had been found, but no one knows where they came from, what their purpose was, nor how long they had been hidden there; they might have been forgotten for years or even been there since the war and were of no further use. Moreover, there are some traces of shooting practice having taken place in the castle a short time ago. Everyone looked at Paolucci with their eyes and mouths wide open; a few were even struck dumb for a few seconds. Most of them left and passed the news on to anyone else they saw. In a few minutes the whole of Klausen knew about it. The news ultimately spread fear and terror; many people believed that the Eisack valley was already in the hands of an armed gang. For the time being, what Paolucci had said caused more and more people spontaneously to decide to hasten to the community center. People, in a fever of expectation, were waiting ever more impatiently for the meeting to begin and for Saverio Zanetti's lecture. Every conversation turned on the anticipated, and most probably scandalous, event. Of course, the Germans did not understand anything about the proceedings. Nevertheless, they found the whole thing highly interesting. They considered the South Tyroleans a very strange people. Incidentally, you now heard them constantly utter—almost as a matter of course—hate-filled statements that were all, in one form or another, directed against foreigners. Sonja Maretsch was standing very close by for a time. What was most repugnant was that the Germans were apparently enjoying themselves all this while; they were conversing quite normally and behaving as though they were interested in this or that and acting with complete good taste. Two ladies, who looked just as though they were having tea in their own homes and feeling extremely comfortable, exchanged remarks like, A: They say they don't stink, but they do stink. B: But Frau Gürtler, who's going to solve the whole problem? By the way, have you actually been to Säben already, the magnificent convent up there? It was a fantastic performance. Someone shouted that Zurner had demanded a summary execution, and Sonja asked what that was supposed to mean, what was to be summarily executed? It was said that the eviction should be summarily carried out. Zurner wanted the castle cleared out; that was why the police had been in action at midday. And why, came the question in response, did he want the castle cleared out? Did he want to knock it down? Some swore that Zurner wanted to knock the castle down, for some reason or other; they even said he wanted to knock it down very soon, he had had enough. That was a phrase that was frequently heard that evening, that *one thing or the other was enough*; it was applied to all sorts of things. A German woman, suddenly and without any reason, said to Sonja Maretsch in the vestibule (of course she did not know Sonja at all): Do you know why I like coming to South Tyrol so much? Sonja: Because . . . of the countryside? She: Yes, the countryside, Oh! the magnificent countryside but, above all, I come here because there are no Turks here. Finally, no Turks. Here, at last, you can breathe again. I tell you I've had enough of them, *et cetera*. As she said this the woman was not looking at Sonja aggressively, but nice and pleasantly, she really seemed to be hoping to have a few nice and pleasant exchanges, culminating in a cozy chat with her, a Klausener. She apparently felt that what she had said to her about the Turks in her homeland was a compliment. If Sonja had mentioned the word *Pakistanis*, she would probably have run away screaming, thrown up in the nearest WC, and then left at once. But enough about the Germans. Finally, a bell rang (Passler, the chairman of the adult education association, rang a small brass bell, that was his practice), an Aha ran through the crowd, and people started moving towards the hall. There was already a crush at the hall door, because everyone wanted to get through the door at the same time. Many people were still holding their glasses and only noticed that they were when they had almost passed through the door; they then turned round again.

Others simply took their glasses with them into the hall. There were no ushers; it had not occurred to anyone to hire any, because for a long time all the events held by the association for adult education had passed off perfectly peacefully and without a largish attendance. Passler, as the chairman of the association, was at first beaming with joy at the great crush; he could already envisage an extraordinarily long article in the *Eisacktaler Tagblatt*, in which, in a day or two's time, this successful event would be reported. The greater the crowd, the longer the article. (The article was ultimately much longer, because of the outrageously scandalous things that took place in the course of the event, and above all, of course, because of the attack that took place in the valley immediately afterwards.) Passler, in his capacity as host, now took a seat near the door to the hall and tried to bring some order into the confusion, but it was obvious that no one was paying any attention to him; the Germans, in fact, looked at him as though all they saw in him was an obstacle and a disruption. Who is this? they said. (In confusion): No idea. It's a South Tyrolean. And what does he want? I don't know, he's just standing around. The South Tyroleans are always standing around, I've noticed that. And a lot of them are alcoholics. Perhaps he wants a groschen *hahaha, et cetera*. A certain lack of restraint spread among all the participants in the event, and the responsibility for this was mainly to be laid at the feet of the Germans who were streaming into the hall in a great crowd. As they knew nothing of what had allegedly happened to Gasser, Badowsky, and the others, they did not act as if they were expecting anything in particular. They entered the hall as though at a theatrical performance. But something had undermined their discipline; it would have been hard to say what. Already at the drinks buffet outside, some of them had grown rather excessively loud; they had been drinking and joking, so that the toboggan was already in motion, and since absolutely nothing got in its way, it began to go faster and faster. As they went into the hall, they shoved the Klauseners away right and left, and groups of them immediately occupied the front rows. If only they had behaved as if they were at a theatrical performance! To tell the truth, they were much more unrestrained, and when the Klauseners in the audience voiced their initial reactions, they at once joined in and gave voice to much stronger comments, even though the whole thing had nothing to do with them. They only did this because they wanted to be entertained and amused. And, in so doing, they revealed a fatal lack of restraint. It could not even be said that they were behaving as they would *at home* in the hall and were letting themselves go. In fact, they let themselves go much more; they didn't care about anything: they threw their tickets all over the place, knocked over their glasses. At first, they were embarrassed, but as the others were doing the same, they soon ceased to be embarrassed any longer, but were even pleased that they were obviously misbehaving, and they were very soon chuckling with pleasure, which was all the more fatal as the Klauseners were taking the whole event very seriously. But here are the details. First of all, Passler came onto the stage, which held nothing but a table and, on the table, a bottle of water, a glass, and a microphone. Next to the table was a projector. All eyes were on Passler, but only for a short, a far too short, time, and then, here and there, a glass was knocked over, and the Germans could be heard whispering something and again chuckling with pleasure. Passler, who did not seem to notice it, surveyed the crowd with a delighted face, for he had never stood in

front of such a large crowd of people before. He had brushed aside
the hostile remarks in the doorway without another thought; perhaps
he had not even noticed them—all he saw in his mind's eye was the
newspaper article and the photo in the *Tagblatt*, and in his mind that
photo was growing bigger and bigger. He now made a gesture as if
he wished to say something, but then something seemed to occur to
him and he disappeared from the stage again. Who was that fellow?
cried one of the Germans. Wasn't he the one who was standing by
the door? What's he doing on the stage? No, he's the lecturer. Aha,
and why has he gone away again? Next the deputy chair of the adult
education association came onto the stage. She was responsible for all
the technical matters. She breathed into the microphone to test it,
then looked at the door of the hall and made a sweeping gesture with
her arm, to indicate that the last visitors were to come in and the
doors were to be closed. A few people sniggered at this movement of
her arm; someone even imitated her, which led to further sniggering.
The woman then made another gesture that meant that the lights
were to be extinguished; the switch was near the door. At the same
time, with exaggerated movements of her lips, she said something
silently to someone who was to operate the switch, probably *lights
off*. Pantomimic gestures of this sort, however, do not go unpunished
before a crowd that is ready to be amused. Laughter could now be
heard from many places, and the gesture in question was imitated, but
this was perhaps not so conspicuous as, in any case, there was a huge
commotion in the hall. Passler now came back onto the stage. Some
people laughed at this for no obvious reason. They probably laughed
simply because Passler appeared on the stage for a second time. They
thought the reason for this was that there had been a mishap: for first

the man appears, then the woman, and now the man again; there must have been a mishap, a hitch in the proceedings that they found amusing. The light was now out; only the stage and the lecturer's table were lit by two spotlights. Passler stood in front, rubbing his hands excitedly, and began (still rubbing his hands) his welcoming speech. Of course he was speaking the Eisack valley dialect. This would generally not have amused any of the Germans, for in their *pensions* they were otherwise very well-behaved and quiet guests who sat there at table at midday and in the evening chatting with their hosts, without behaving conspicuously in any way. But now they found themselves in a large group and the mood had already grown very expansive. The toboggan was now traveling at full speed. Some were laughing at Passler, others were smiling to themselves; they obviously considered Passler's adult education association a sort of cage in a zoo with particularly grotesque kinds of animals in it. The Klauseners, on the other hand, were all seized by a strange tension; they listened most attentively to Passler's opening words, completely meaningless as they were. Ladies and gentlemen, he said, my dear Klauseners, my dear members of the adult education association . . . (short pause, a sweeping gesture with his arms) . . . my dear guests here in Klausen, I would like to welcome you most heartily to another evening in our lecture series on South Tyrolean culture. Many of you will perhaps remember the last lecture when our dear Dr. Pfundnei-der . . . *et cetera*. Passler was already saying too much. Pfundneider, the name made people laugh, but in a puzzling way Passler was talk-ing with an expression of truly warm-hearted pleasure and enthusi-asm on his face, although most people found what he was saying boring and out of place, for no one wanted to know anything about

Pfundneider's lecture, to which, in any case, only about fifteen people had come. Passler really did cut an involuntarily comic figure: he
was very tall, was slightly humpbacked, his face was bent forward
like a bird's, and he looked at his audience with a frightfully ingenu-
ous look—a look which was reinforced by his bushy, downward slant-
ing eyebrows. It seemed that he had to hold his eyes open by force.
And as he stood there rubbing his hands and bending forwards, his
ill-fitting clothes hung higgledy-piggledy on him. What a character,
said the Germans. They seemed to be concentrating more, for now
the presentation had apparently started. For no reason at all, Passler
was now talking himself into a state of real enthusiasm; he was praising the province and its people, pointing out Klausen's magnificent
situation (obviously he was saying all of this for the benefit of the
tourists), people were always in a *good mood* in the Eisack valley, he
claimed, and then—without any motivation—shouted things like
Let's be off then! and *Let's go merrily onward forever!* People thought he
was now finished and would finally start to talk about the lecture
that he was due to announce. But Passler now started to praise South
Tyrolean wine, the age-old Vernatsch, the Lagrein, and, first and
foremost, the Sylvaner, and, in his enthusiasm, he shouted to the
audience, anyone who has tasted the Eisack valley Sylvaner will remain an optimist all his life. He was saying all this nonsense simply
to call attention to the drinks buffet and to invite everyone to have a
glass of wine after the lecture, although most of the guests had already served themselves. Probably, Passler simply wanted to be as
hospitable as possible to the tourists because they had come to the
lecture in such numbers. This was doubtless the reason for his making this unsuitable speech, which half the audience found astonishing

and boring and the other half merely laughable. Incidentally, some people had still not taken their places; the order to close the door had been given much too soon. The door kept being opened from outside, people were pushing their way into rows of seats that were already almost full, and others were standing by the walls—the hall became more and more crowded. Everyone was there. Old Moreth and young Moreth were to be seen, both of them standing; Taschner was sitting not far from them; Perluttner in turn near him. Huber was there; Valli, Meraner and his group of regulars; Neri was sitting, all on his own, further back. The professor could be seen fairly far forward. Paolucci was also present, together with a photographer; the whole of the Maretsch family; the Grubers; Nussbaumer and his wife; even the mayor was there. Delazer was standing right at the back; he had just arrived. He was leaning against the wall with his arms folded and his legs crossed, obviously quite detached—he seemed almost amused. A lot of people were looking at him; a murmur even ran round the hall when, in spite of the half light at the back of the hall, which at first made it hard to distinguish people's faces clearly, he was recognized. Passler was now talking about the lecturer. He was delighted, he said, to welcome such a profound authority as Herr Zanetti M.A. to the adult education association in the Klausen community center this evening, *et cetera, et cetera*. He followed this up with Zanetti's *curriculum vitae*. Zanetti was twenty-eight years old, had studied in Florence, Paris, and Berlin and had also lived in those cities for some time, said Passler again extremely ingenuously, and was thus a widely traveled man and it was particularly delightful that he had found himself in our beautiful South Tyrol at the University of Bolzano and has come up here to Klausen to give us a lecture this evening. He went on talking and talking, it went on for minutes, for he started over and over again with this and that, although everything he said consisted of totally empty phrases. And now, said Passler, clear the stage for our lecturer, I rejoice and you, honored guests, rejoice with me. Please! With that he left the stage. But he returned to the stage immediately, for a second time, with a much more devoted and friendly look and cried: But I forgot to tell you what we are going to hear today, although you already know it from the placards, but I will repeat it, so that everyone here will know . . . our good Herr Zanetti M.A. is speaking to us this evening about . . . (he now had a piece of paper in his hand) . . . Your attention please! it is important that I repeat this, because . . . (the audience had by now lost all patience) . . . because this announcement is no longer correct, it has now transpired that Herr Doktor Zanetti (the former M.A. had now become a Ph.D.) . . . is not going to speak to us this evening about the local economic space and its culture and so on but is going to make a very well-known person more accessible to us, a German philosopher whose name is probably very familiar to us all, for we also have in Klausen an, even if I cannot see him just at this moment . . . (he was now in a complete muddle). Someone: What's the title of the lecture then? Another man: Why isn't he talking about the economy? A third: We were expecting something about the problems. We expected something about the problems! He should speak about the problems. Passler looked at the audience through half-closed eyes. He had no idea what problems people were suddenly talking about. Well, he said, that's how it's turned out . . . the scholar . . . sometimes changes his subject . . . but we are eagerly looking forward to a lecture on the topic (reading energetically):

Ontology and Consciousness. Hypotheses about Heidegger.

And with this, Passler was finally off the stage. A number of people stood up, surprised, and gave vent to their displeasure because—they could not understand what it was all about, they felt insecure. And now, inexplicably, the light came on again, no one could say why. The Germans sitting in the front rows were confused and did not know how to react. The Klauseners on the other hand were arguing. We are not interested in this ontology, or whatever it's called! someone shouted quite loudly. Then someone said, It doesn't matter what the title is, it is more important for this Zanetti to speak: in that way we shall also gain enlightenment, for he'll say something about the whole matter, we can be sure of that. (A lot of people had been using these vague expressions and talking of *the whole matter* or *the event as a whole*, for they could not express anything in concrete terms; they were just constantly awaiting something, even if it was certainly not what eventually occurred). Incidentally, all the chaotic scenes that followed in the instant after Passler's speech of welcome and his introduction of the speaker were only possible because Saverio Zanetti did not appear on the stage quickly enough. That is to say, he did not in fact appear on the stage at all for the time being. Nothing happened for several minutes, no one came onto the stage, everyone was talking, and then the lights went out again, but without Zanetti's having appeared. People kept on talking in the semi-darkness. While the Germans, in the front, were starting to grow more aggressive again and began cursing the event and demanding, at the top of their voices, that at least they should pour them out the wine that had been promised if there wasn't going to be a lecture, suddenly a few totally

unknown people were standing in the back rows among the Klauseners. These unknown people bore no resemblance to the tourists
in the front rows. The tourists in the front of the hall were exclusively either groups of senior citizens or married couples. No one,
afterwards, could say where the unknown people had suddenly come
from. It seemed to many people that they had seen one or the other
of them that afternoon at the demonstration in front of Ploder castle,
but that could have been sheer imagination. The unknown people at
the back were strangely inconspicuous in spite of their undisciplined
appearance. (Later on, no one could any longer say whether there
was just one group of them or whether several groups had been roaming around Klausen. It was never fully resolved). And now several
things happened all at once; they were all completely unexpected, but
they did not attract any further attention, although they did look
very strange and were later of great interest to the police. The Germans had become quite noisy again, and the atmosphere had become
very heated; they were all ready to get up and leave, but someone up
at the front persuaded them that it would be better to stay, the lecture
would surely start soon, it was certain to be eventful, he himself was
all agog. The person speaking was the one who, at the beginning of
Passler's welcoming speech, had laughed especially loudly and brash-
ly and had made as much noise as possible with his glass, so that the
rest of them had also grown more and more restless. This person now
suddenly stood up and walked to the back. It was Badowsky. This
time he was not in his shirtsleeves, but was wearing a jacket, and his
hair was combed to one side in a strange manner. That was why he
had gone unrecognized all that time. Later, many people said that he
had mixed with the Germans intentionally, so as to create as restless

a mood as possible. If that really had been his plan, then it was a total success. Now he went to the back and suddenly disappeared between the partitions. But he went straight back to the front, for now something else happened. Gasser appeared. He was standing there at the back, by the wall, and was looking into the hall with a very strange expression on his face, as concentrated as it was confused. At first no one saw him. Then Badowsky recognized him. Badowsky was about to approach him, but then frowned and paused, without taking his eyes off Gasser. The latter noticed none of this. Now, finally, Zanetti entered the hall. All eyes followed him as, with his manuscript in his hands, he walked past the rows of seats, and because everyone was watching only him, Gasser remained almost completely unnoticed. He looked around and noticed Badowsky. Badowsky once more made as if to approach him, but immediately stopped again, as Gasser made a deterring gesture with his hand, though he did not look in Badowsky's direction. Badowsky appeared somewhat perplexed and looked at his watch. (It was later hard for the people who had seen all this to reconstruct it. Of course what was happening could either mean everything or nothing. However, later on—for a long time— many people became strangely tense whenever they recalled the moment). The next instant Gasser had already disappeared again, perhaps not even through a door at the back but through the door to the hall, without anyone having noticed, for the door still kept on opening and shutting at frequent intervals. The unknown people had also suddenly disappeared, and so had Badowsky. Zanetti was now at last at the front, on the stage. People had been waiting almost ten minutes for him; Passler was sitting there very anxiously. Then, however, he sprang up, went up onto the stage, and said that Herr Dr.

Zanetti was now here, and would like to apologize for the short delay; *But let's always go merrily onwards* and *let's get down to work, et cetera.* He then sat down again. Zanetti took his seat, adjusted his chair, looked for a moment at the projector that had been set up unnecessarily, then rather fussily arranged his manuscript. After that, he looked interestedly at the crowded audience and cleared his throat. Finally, someone shouted. (Confusion): So, the other man wasn't the speaker. No, this is the speaker. And who was the other one, *et cetera.* Zanetti noticed the general restlessness and looked sternly at the audience, perhaps a little too sternly, as some found it arrogant. Then he cleared his throat again. The tension had reached its height, everyone was awaiting Zanetti's opening words. Ladies and gentlemen, he began, esteemed members . . . But he got no further. Alderman Moreth took a few steps towards the front and shouted: Herr Zanetti, it is said that you are a member of what I would call in the broadest sense, a political association, which has set as its goal, very concretely . . . to attack, in general, certain conditions in our country and our society . . . actually our civilization as a whole . . . with all the means at your disposal. What do you mean by that? asked Zanetti, obviously completely taken aback. Well, shouted Moreth, while his son looked at him aghast, for Moreth was terribly red in the face, which, given the diffuse light, seemed even more threatening than usual, well, is it not true that you have made statements in public, here in Klausen, that attack our trade and our economy as a whole and depict them both as the work of the devil? Possibly, that is the object of the present meeting, possibly you wish to spread those views here as well? Zanetti: As the devil's work? Ladies and gentlemen, I'm afraid I do not understand. Who is talking about the devil? But that is—please let us get this right—that is childish. Why should I resort to such childishness? Perluttner jumped up and shouted angrily, The devil is not childishness! All his life he had not only feared the devil, but had even, in the main, ordered his life as he had because of this fear, his life was not a sham. It was not a sham, but if he was now asserting that the devil was just childishness, then he was maintaining that his, Perluttner's, life was a sham. (Someone): I never did believe these economic prophets. (The shout was apparently completely unmotivated). Perluttner now rushed quite senselessly to the front and shook his fist over his head, as though he were absolutely determined to threaten someone with it or even scare them. But, I admit, I used to believe in these economic prophets, but that was earlier, and so now I say to you: I am against them. Enough, I am totally opposed to them. I am against this sort of economy. I am . . . I am against it. Moreth: The economy's there, so it's not debatable. What is there to change in the economy, it cannot be changed, it goes its own way, it is like a . . . a natural law. You have to comply with it, there's no other way. My God, be glad that we have this progress. Some people burst into laughter at this. Zanetti was sitting at his table at the front of the podium looking out into the audience, as astonished as he was amused. I do not understand, he said, why these subjects . . . Meraner suddenly jumped up as well. He pointed at Zanetti with his arm outstretched and cried: What do you mean, you don't understand? You yourself have incited people! You have incited people and now, of course, you deny it, that's all a part of your scheming and of your tactics overall, denying it afterwards. Zanetti: Whom have I incited? And to do what, what have I incited people to do? I simply do not understand what you are talking about. Do you have any reason for saying so? Please explain yourself, it is really distressing to have to sit up here while . . . Frau Maretsch: What are these forbidden books that everyone is talking about everywhere? Zanetti now appeared astonished beyond all measure. He seemed not to have thought that his whole character would be subjected to this in public. How do you know about that? he stammered. For a moment it really looked as though he was losing his composure, but perhaps it was just a trick, according to a prearranged plan, because who, except for him, could have spread the rumor that he had anything to do with such books? Well, he replied, in my profession, I have to read such books, but I do not know what you have been told. It is my scholarly job to read certain books, and I tell you, be glad that you . . . he was about to say that you yourself do not have to read such books. But it was obviously all lies. It was utterly improbable that Zanetti, in his academic discipline and his special subject, had anything to do with books on the Index. However, people immediately believed him when he said that he was concerned with these books because of his scholarly discipline and not merely on his own initiative (which would have been the truth), but the atmosphere did not improve because of this: it only became worse, because people now considered the whole branch of learning represented by Zanetti suspect and dangerous. Someone cried out that people like the Italians, with their pessimism, just wanted to cause trouble. Even Huber now shouted a quite unmotivated statement to the crowd (though it seemed quite logical to him at that moment): You are not going to destroy our handicraft here, our handicraft is not going to be destroyed! Valli said, Trade and traffic, it was well known, had always made for prosperity, everyone wants to be involved in trade and traffic. But this involvement is not always advantageous. There are times when you have to talk about the disadvantages. About what disadvantages? someone demanded. Another man: I am a woodworker. I work with wood, I have a sawmill up in Karnol. Tell me, what would my business be without the autobahn? It would be nothing. No one knew why this man from Karnol suddenly started talking about the autobahn; obviously he thought people had been talking about the autobahn all the time. I have customers all the way to Trient, he shouted, and what am I to do about them? Someone: Your father used to own the sawmill and he didn't have customers all the way to Trient, he didn't have customers any further away than Bolzano and Sterzing, but in those days people also used to pay something, today they don't want to pay any more. (Confusion): What's he talking about? Is he one of the people from the action group? It ought to be banned, the action group. (Others): Unfortunately you can't ban anything in a democracy. Anyone can malign anybody in a democracy, that's democracy, that's precisely what it is. (More confusion.) We don't let ourselves be abused and insulted here, we are decent people, they can't do that sort of thing to us. Oh! Bullshit! cried the opposition, nobody's being insulted, but things can't go on this way. (Counter-cry): We built this up with our own hands. We've always worked honestly. (Others): Herr Delazer should say something about it. Mr. Architect, say something about it and about your boss, Herr Laner! (A student): There is no honest work any more. Our century is traffic tailbacks, monopoly, lack of transparency. Everyone was shouting at the same time, everyone was expressing a different point of view, and no one had any idea what was being talked about. Zanetti was leaning back in his armchair at the front of the podium, his arms folded, and was obviously pleased with the outcome of the event. It did not look as though he was about to present any hypotheses about Heidegger's hypotheses. (How had he hit upon Heidegger? Possibly it was just a truly diabolical trick.) But now something completely unexpected happened. Someone came rushing in; no one took any notice at first. It was Gruber's brother. He said something that at first no one could understand, because there was too much noise in the hall and no one grew any quieter, even when he began shouting the words *police* and *bridge* because, as no one was listening to him, everyone thought it was just one more vocal contribution to the general chaos. Listen, he shouted, just listen to me! but it was pointless. Everyone kept carrying on noisily shouting something or other. Then Gruber, who had managed to fight his way through to his brother and the two Maretschs, was saying very excitedly, but with an almost exalted facial expression, that the police were outside, that there was something going on up on the other side of the valley, that Auer was said to be on the autobahn for some reason, and that someone had seen him there. At this, the two Grubers and the Maretsch siblings left the hall without anyone following them. Something else, certainly completely unexpected, then happened outside the hall. Gasser, namely, was sitting around out there. He had not been seen since the nights up at Ploder castle: he was reckoned to have disappeared. Even beforehand in the hall they had not noted his presence, and now he was simply sitting there on a chair by the wall. In any case, he was in an extremely sad state. When Marestch spoke to him he scarcely replied. When asked where he had been all the time, he said nothing. He looked very exhausted and above all completely listless, he just kept on making defensive gestures with his hand and staring right through everybody in a strange way. When his look grew firmer, it was obviously only by a great effort on his part. Gasser gave the impression of having taken the weight of the world on his shoulders in the preceding days and of having completely collapsed under this weight. Sonja said later that she had seen Gasser in this state on a few previous occasions but that on this occasion she had seen right away that he was obviously in a most alarming state. This all remained most puzzling. Maretsch asked whether he, Gasser, knew what was happening with Auer. Gasser appeared disoriented and said he had seen Auer a few hours earlier in his room above the Cellar but that Auer had been very drunk, very drunk. He had shown him the new pictures. Gasser's eyes lit up for a moment when he recalled Auer's pictures (he meant his drawings), but then his eyes began once more—but even more strangely this time—to stare right through everything. They will hate him for them, he said. Maretsch looked at him, somewhat taken aback. Then Maretsch asked: Did you write this notice that is pasted up all over the place today? No, said Gasser, he had not written anything. Why should he write anything? Maretsch: You know nothing about it? And that business with Zurner, what was that about Zurner? Some people suppose that that had something to do with you. Has it got anything to do with you? Gasser: With me? It's an interesting guess, certainly. Incidentally that's all really uncalled for, and that's what I thought that same night. Maretsch: Which night? Gasser: The night when everyone was up at Ploder castle. The Italian went on talking forever. It was unbearable. There came a point when I couldn't stand the Italian's prattle any longer. Everything was empty and completely superfluous. Maretsch: What was superfluous? Do be more explicit. But Gasser was talking very confusedly. He obviously had no interest in giving any explicit answers, or else he was not in a state to do so. He soon turned away and left the building. The others followed him, also confused. It was only then that it once more occurred to them that something had happened in the valley, for there really were two police vans standing outside. The fact that there were two of them at once was indeed unusual. Something strange was going on outside, but the people there could not immediately grasp what it was. A change had taken place, something was completely different from what it had been earlier. At first it seemed to them as though the wind had freshened, that seemed the obvious explanation. Gruber and Maretsch looked at each other inquiringly. The policemen stood mutely by, staring up at the sky the whole time. They also seemed surprised. Can you hear it? asked Gasser. Everyone was trying to listen. There really was nothing to hear. There was a dead silence. The group stood there puzzled. Maretsch even clasped his hands for a moment and put them to his mouth. Now young Moreth came out of the building, looked at Gasser and the others in utter astonishment, and was then also suddenly still. Why is it so quiet out here? he asked. This brought everyone to their senses. They walked a few steps to the riverbank and looked across the river up to the bridge over the valley. There was nothing there. Everything was quiet. There were no cars, no trucks. Maretsch said later, at that moment, he really thought that a miracle had happened, an awesome law of nature had suddenly been suspended. Something unfathomable had happened. Everyone was holding their breath; there were even tears in Sonja's and her brother's eyes. Silence in Klausen. Nothing had ever sounded more unimaginable than that. Silence in Klausen. Then other people came out of the community center . . . Maretsch made a hissing sound to silence them. What's happened over there? one of them cried. And now the whole bank quickly filled with people coming out of the community center. There, up there, someone shouted and pointed across the river. There really were two men in overalls, or sports clothes, under the piers of the viaduct. They were doing something there, but at that distance it was impossible to make out what, everything was very small. A third man suddenly lowered himself on a rope from above, straight off the road; he seemed very expert in rappelling and quickly covered several meters right on one of the massive piers. Then he stopped and started doing something at a spot on the pier. It all happened very quickly and in dead silence. Up there! someone shouted, look up there, who's that? Someone was standing up above on the shoulder of the road and seemed to be waving at the Klauseners down on the riverbank. He was waving like a madman, in the way children wave at passing cars from the bridge over the autobahn. Then suddenly other people could be seen; they came running up and pulled the man who was waving to one side—it looked as though a scuffle was taking place. Now, everything happened all at once. The process was choreographed like an absurd ballet and was moreover completely silent because of the great distance. The person on the pier had now rappelled down, wriggled out of his straps and run away to the left with the other two men. They ran up the slope and disappeared into the thicket. As it was beginning to get darker, it was impossible to make anything out with any clarity, but the haziness and the damp atmosphere lent the proceedings a certain theatrical quality. All the people on one side of the Eisack were silent; many were holding their breath and were looking absolutely mesmerized at what was happening on the other bank. At the place where, until recently, the people in overalls or sports clothes had been (the opponents of globalization, the terrorists, or protectors of the environment as they were later called: the words were used as needed), carabinieri appeared after a few minutes and searched the whole area. After a time, while everyone continued to watch the scene on the opposite side of the valley, an explosion was suddenly heard. It was not loud; quite the contrary, it was a low sound, but strangely muffled. All the people on the other bank looked at one another. What was that? they asked. Something exploded! someone shouted. An explosion, an explosion! someone now screamed out loud. A tumult arose, and everyone started running; they scattered in panic in all directions. That did it, Klausen was now a crime scene.

It was still night when the first television crews arrived. Some commentators were to be seen standing on the bank of the Eisack or in the upper part of the town giving their reports while the cameras were rolling. In the following days, the town grew fuller and fuller, hardly had one television crew departed when the next one appeared. Almost every Klausener who approached the journalists was hauled in front of the camera to say a few words or, if he had nothing to say, at least to announce how shocked he was. On the morning after the events, Gasser was interviewed twice; he gave the interviews with great enthusiasm, but what he said was so very confused that no one could make head or tail of it. In the early afternoon, Gasser, Maretsch, and Gruber were all arrested, at almost the same time, in a very hectic operation. A few hours later, Auer—who had run away after the scuffle on the bridge, that is, he hadn't actually run away, he had just been totally drunk and had been roaming about in the woods on the eastern side of the valley for more than twenty hours after the event—was also picked up. Paolucci was arrested towards evening, and Zanetti was taken during the night. Badowsky was not to be found; he had probably escaped over the border into Austria. Photographs of all these things, that is a total of six arrests, could be seen on television that same night, and on the following days, throughout Europe and even as far away as the USA. The overall impression was that a large, highly disciplined terrorist organization had been taken prisoner at one fell swoop. True, Gruber and Maretsch were let go in the course of the first night—no one in Klausen could really understand why the carbinieri had arrested the two of them in the first place, since no one had had any suspicions of them. Paolucci, too, was released on the following day (he boasted about his night in jail for months afterwards, as though it were a trophy). Zanetti was held longer. When his house was searched, certain papers and also some illicit pornographic materials were found, and charges were brought about the latter. He was never seen in Klausen again. This left only two members of the terrorist gang, Auer and Gasser. It is remarkable that the whole western world paid so much attention to what had happened in Klausen. Terrorists (ecologists) blow up a bridge over the autobahn, the world had yet to see anything like it, this was something new. However, as it quickly transpired, the operation had been carried out in a more than amateurish fashion, and the bridge over the valley had not been seriously damaged. That is, it was not damaged at all; all that happened was that a toolshed on the slope near the autobahn had exploded and even that was not really the right expression—there was just a small explosion, and the completely ramshackle shed then burned out without anyone having suffered

any harm. At first Gasser was thought to be the person behind the
operation. A detailed sketch of the autobahn viaduct had been found
in his coat. The sketch was to be seen in the newspaper; Perluttner
testified that Gasser had made it three weeks beforehand, sitting on
the bench in front of the church, that he had watched him doing it
and had told Gasser's mother. Furthermore, a five-page handwritten
document was found: it was about Ploder castle, the situation of its
residents, and the quarrel between Alois Zurner and Minister Laner
over the castle. The newspaper article about the protests by the Society for the Protection of Birds against the searchlight at the Sam was
also found. That was enough to form a picture right there and then!
A series of numbers had been written in the margin of the newspaper
article; this turned out to be the phone number of the Piedmontese
woman who lived at Branzoll, *et cetera, et cetera*. Everything became
a link in an impressive chain; for a few days, people were convinced
by all of it and considered it quite conclusive: Gasser and the brutal
attack on Zurner (the light gun!) . . . Gasser and his contacts with
Ploder castle (the weapon store, target practice) . . . Gasser and the
attack on the autobahn (the sketch made in front of the church) . . .
Gasser's absence for several days (according to Sonja, however, not
unusual) . . . finally: Gasser's hatred of Delazer, his envy of his sister,
et cetera, et cetera . . . Witnesses' statements, the contents of which
follow, were made about the happenings on the bridge. At first it was
said that, before the attack, several persons—dressed like ordinary
road-workers—had come from the north and the south onto the affected segment of the A22, and they had stopped the traffic with
official-looking signals and had used barriers to block the road. Meanwhile, it was alleged that several people had attempted to stretch a

banner between two of the bridge's massive piers, but that this had failed for some reason, one side of it having fallen into the river. The banner was later found: it bore a slogan that was against transit traffic; the slogan was in very general terms, without direct reference either to the situation in the Eisack valley or in Klausen. People on the road had not been able to see any of this. At some point, one of the men is said to have taken off his work-clothes and begun rappelling down the bridge. Another man (Auer) was said to have suddenly stood in the middle of the road, gesticulating wildly with his hands, then he seemed to be making a speech, but it could not be discerned to whom the speech was addressed; he simply stood around and talked and talked and with great verve. He was completely drunk, no one, incidentally, could say how he had come to show up on the bridge across the valley—presumably he had intended to spend the night in the toolshed, alone with a bottle of schnapps, and so had seen the arrival of the activists or terrorists at close quarters and had let himself be inveigled into taking part in an incomprehensible action, i.e., to walk on the autobahn. Both to the north and the south of the closed-off section, the occupants of trucks and automobiles were by this time getting out to find out why the road had been closed without prior notice, and above all what this strange chap was doing on the road. Some were blowing their horns, but only for a short time. Since the road behind the barrier could not be seen, many people assumed that something had happened behind the angle of the hill, an accident, an avalanche, a rock slide, *et cetera*. Discussions with the people in work-clothes began. They said very little; the truck-drivers, on the other hand, soon grew aggressive, saying that they were losing money while they were standing around. The people in work-

clothes were not only men but also women and even girls, but this
had not, at first, aroused anyone's suspicion. What was more suspicious, however, was that the people in (Italian) road-workers' clothes
were obviously all German and French, and even Dutch. The truck-
drivers, after having been stopped for a few minutes, had grown so
aggressive that they were just about to get rough; some of them were
already starting to move the barriers themselves or kick them angrily
off the road. They had a right to an open road! they shouted. No one
could close the road to them, in any case, there was too much construction, there was always construction, but this construction only
existed because the authorities had nothing to do and just sent out
their workmen to do unnecessary things—for no other reason than
that of uselessness. Strikingly, all the people in work-clothes suddenly disappeared at that moment, as though on a signal (possibly
something had not gone according to plan, and so they had gone off
the road in an easterly direction and dispersed in the woods); only
Auer remained behind. In a few seconds, the truck drivers and the
car drivers were at his side. For a few moments, Auer obviously still
found what was happening here comical, but the truck drivers, especially, were ready to lynch him. They did not even ask what he was
doing there on the road (as if he owned it!) but immediately seized
him by the collar, threw him to the ground, kicked him right across
the road, and threw him a couple of meters down into the ditch, simply because they thought that he (Auer) had wanted to prevent them
from driving. Don't prevent us from driving! they shouted. Don't
prevent us from driving! Several of them also shouted: I'll kill you if
you prevent me from driving again! (Others): We won't put up with
it, no way will we put up with people preventing us from driving!

Then they cleared the last barriers away, went to their cars and their trucks, started their engines, and drove off before the carbinieri had arrived on the scene. With this, quiet in Klausen had passed. The people on the road were in such a rage that they had obviously paid no attention to the explosion. Even when they saw the shed burning, they didn't think it had anything to do with them; they simply drove on. Just a few truck drivers remained behind and offered themselves to the carabinieri as witnesses. No one ever discovered who the people in work-clothes were. At first, almost everyone thought it was a group that Gasser had called into being, supported financially by the woman from Piedmont, and that the whole plan to blow up the bridge had been concocted up at Branzoll; many even considered the owner of Branzoll to be the intellectual force behind it, since it was known that, because of the autobahn, she kept all the windows and shutters on the eastern side of her castle closed (people had always regarded this with suspicion; the fact that she always made such a point of keeping her shutters closed was considered almost as an insult to the whole town of Klausen). But in the end, no one had been able to prove anything against her and Gasser. The only thing that the public prosecutor could base a case on was the aforementioned drawing. Later no one knew what part Gasser had played in the event; it was not even certain that he had played any part at all. For a long while it was asserted, here and there, that Gasser must have known, at least in part, of the projected operation, perhaps from Badowsky or from somebody or other in Berlin. The business with the explosives also remained baffling. There was a definite theory that perhaps the explosives had been placed up there in the toolshed by completely different people, for completely different purposes; possibly one of the activists (or Auer) had simply thrown a cigarette into the shed, nothing more. It was also never proven that the holes that were found in the pier were really holes for the insertion of dynamite. After a while, even the carabinieri did not consider that a probability. Similar holes were to found everywhere in the piers, and above all, why had the explosives obviously not been attached? Was that a fault in the planning, a failure in the course of the operation, or had they only wished to block the autobahn for a short moment and unroll their banner with the slogan on it . . . for a short, a very short, moment of peace? Had there, in the end, never been a plan to blow up the bridge at all? Had the explosives in the shed been forgotten for years? When this theory was made public in Klausen, a lot of people appeared really dissatisfied, even disappointed. What! They didn't intend to blow up the bridge? Of course they intended to blow up the bridge . . . nothing was more evident than that it was to have been blown up, *et cetera* . . . People then seized on the parcel with the black and red characters that had been found by the lime silo, but there were absolutely no clues there either. Neri suddenly said that he could not exactly recall the parcel he saw in Gasser's hands, perhaps he had had a completely different parcel with him when he came down from Branzoll, perhaps it was only a paper bag, and perhaps there were only garden tools in the bags, his, Neri's, eyes were bad, it was just that, in that first instant he had thought . . . because you could read about it in all the papers and he had seen the pictures as well. Sensation seekers even began appearing in the town; they took over the hotels and, standing on the bank of the river, had the viaduct pointed out to them and the event explained to them (or they were led to believe it was being explained) in the most assorted versions and accompanied by the widest ranging theories. Then there was an expert opinion: The intention really was to blow up two piers, but the terrorists had made a mistake, and the man who had rappelled down was to have corrected something on the pier that could, however, no longer be corrected, so the terrorists had left again, taking all their technical equipment with them. A lot of Klauseners clapped their hands; the tours to the riverbank were intensified. In any case, what the report contained seemed highly improbable. It was followed by other, very contradictory, reports. The most varied suspicions were voiced. (Against Paolucci as well; it was maintained that, a few months previously, he had made Zanetti's acquaintance and had met with him on several occasions in Bologna.) A great deal of confusion was created in this way. It was asserted that Zanetti's lecture and the disturbance that Badowsky had created had been part of the plan and served as a diversion. It was said that rumors had been spread beforehand in order to create anxiety in Klausen, to collect the people in the community center and thus keep them away from the scene of the action. As for the shot: it was later persistently claimed that at the time of the event a shot was also heard (people said so because everyone was talking about it), but no one could be found who had actually heard the shot or actually seen the shooter, besides which there was no victim; but in spite of this, for a time, the theory that Gasser had wanted to use the confusion, or had even staged it, in order to fire off a well-directed shot at Delazer across the Eisack, still endured. When people were reminded that Gasser had been standing on the riverbank the whole time and had not stirred from the spot (in order to fire the shot from the other side), many people replied that Gasser, in the middle of executing the plan he had concocted earlier, had suddenly given it up; why, of course, they did not say. The non-execution of the plan was for them a perfectly logical indication that just such a plan existed. In short: no one knew what had actually happened on the day in question, what had happened by chance, what had taken place deliberately. Close scrutiny revealed that the event resolved itself into a cosmos of possibilities, but if you considered it from a distance, everything was quite clear and even simple. Indeed, to this day, most people believe that six terrorists (Gasser, Gruber, Maretsch and the others) had blown up or had intended to blow up the A22 . . . That same night the police broke into Auer's room. The *pazzi*, the drawings of the Klauseners that Auer had done, were hanging all over the walls. They were all to be seen: Moreth, Valli, Pareith, Gruber, Kerschbaumer, Huber, the Mayor, Neri, Meraner, Meraner's wife, Gasser, Gasser's father, Gasser's mother, Kati, Paolucci, Laner, Delazer, Pfundneider, Passler; they were all hanging there in an attitude that suggested that they were tethered, and were suffering the torments of their own, individual eternal punishments of hell; instruments of torture were, however, not to be seen, all that could be seen were the torments in the expressions of their faces and their souls. Incidentally there were also portraits of the Chief Minister and the Minister of Transport . . . Above the single tiny little window in this room hung a piece of paper and on it a handwritten note of Auer's, a quotation. There, underlined several times, stood the strange words: *Let me draw a hideous face, a hideous face with a wide-open mouth!*

A ndreas Maier was born in Bad Nauheim outside Frankfurt in 1967. In addi-tion to winning the Ernst Willner Prize at the Ingeborg Bachmann Literary Competition in Klagenfurt, Austria, in 2000, he received the Jürgen Ponto Foundation's Literary Support Prize and the Aspekte Literary Prize for his first novel, *Wäldchestag*.

Kenneth J. Northcott is professor emeritus of German at the University of Chicago. He has translated many books, among them Thomas Bernhard's *The Voice Imitator*, *Histrionics*, and *Three Novellas*.

Open Letter—the University of Rochester's nonprofit, literary translation press—is one of only a handful of publishing houses dedicated to increasing access to world literature for English readers. Publishing ten titles in translation each year, Open Letter searches for works that are extraordinary and influential, works that we hope will become the classics of tomorrow.

Making world literature available in English is crucial to opening our cultural borders, and its availability plays a vital role in maintaining a healthy and vibrant book culture. Open Letter strives to cultivate an audience for these works by helping readers discover imaginative, stunning works of fiction and by creating a constellation of international writing that is engaging, stimulating, and enduring.

Current and forthcoming titles from Open Letter include works from Catalonia, France, Iceland, Russia, South Africa, and numerous other countries.

www.openletterbooks.org